Make Believe

The Hexford Witches
Book One

C.B. Hallam

This edition published by Salpe Publishing
2024.

ISBN: 978-1-0686533-0-8

CONTENTS

1	Chapter Name	1
2	Chapter Name	178
3	Chapter Name	181

Chapter One

Dust motes danced on a beam of pale Yorkshire sunlight that cut across the cottage kitchen. With moss green painted cabinets and natural wood worktops, the room was an extension of the forest outside. Centuries of use were evident in the little scratches and stains of the well-loved kitchen. A large black range, as old as Kallin Beck cottage itself, had a newer gas cooker beside it. The fridge, too, was modern but blended in well with all the chintzy fridge magnets and trinkets dangling from its door. And at the centre island, by a robust old table perfectly balanced on the flagstones, Dinah Nye worked.

Taking a handful of flour from a hessian bag, she

spread it on the surface, swiping her hand lovingly across the wood. With her thumb placed at the centre of the flour patch, she extended her little finger and used it as a compass to draw a circle in the flour. Dinah touched the circle top and bottom, left and right, pushing a little of her concentration into each movement, knowing that the table, the kitchen, and the cottage itself were already aligned to the cardinal directions. A heavy ceramic bowl went into the centre of her circle and into that she added her ingredients. With two eggs she paused for a moment, cupping them as if to warm them before cracking them on the bowl's edge and releasing the contents with a deft motion. Adding flour by the handful, letting her hard-earned wisdom and instincts guide her more than any recipe, she formed a shaggy dough with her fingers. An ancient apron protected the complex floral print of her dress. From the tips of her fingers to the rolled sleeves of her oversized cardigan, her arms were white with flour, only a few shades lighter than her own pale skin. Her mousey hair was tied into a loose ponytail, but it did very little to stop one annoying strand of hair from tickling her face as she worked the dough. She huffed at it to no effect and then used the back of her hand to brush it aside, smearing flour across her freckles.

Setting the bowl aside, flour puffed across the table's surface again and Dinah bore down on the fresh dough. Her attention was rapt on the dough, her mind focussed on making this batch of scones good. They would be tasty. They would be solid but light. And anyone who tasted them would instantly feel like they were home. That was the intent which she poured into every fold.

Working the dough, she didn't notice her housemate enter. In fact, Eshe Morgan managed to enter, take the milk from the fridge, boil the kettle, and make two cups of tea before Dinah looked up, her eyes refocusing on the present only when there were thirteen dough pucks coated in fresh egg yolk on the baking tray.

Eshe smiled from behind her round glasses, her dark skin and eyes warm with sincerity and bright with her ravenous intelligence. Her black hair was a short blow out with a perpendicular parting. She looked every bit the student with her white shirt tucked into the buckle of her jeans and one of her many knitted vests over the top.

"Good morning," Eshe said with a faint lilt of Welsh in her voice.

"Hi," Dinah said, with a smile as broad as her Yorkshire accent. "This batch is going to be really good."

"Every batch is good. Great, in fact." Eshe slurped her tea and motioned to Dinah's beside her.

"Ooh. Thank you." Dinah scooped up the tea in two floury hands, as if the mug wasn't blisteringly hot, and took a sip; her baker's hands impervious to ovens and hot beverages. "I'm off to work in a bit, but I wanted to get this fresh batch ready to deliver on the way. Are you poking the cottage today?"

Eshe became a little serious. "Every time I peel back a layer of sigils, I find another underneath. Did I tell you that I found a little clay frog tucked under the cornerstone the other day?"

"Did you put it back?" Dinah asked.

"Didn't take it out in the first place. He looked pretty happy under there."

Dinah chuckled, sliding the baking tray into the hot oven. "I've told you, the cottage likes being enigmatic."

Eshe held up a hand to her friend. "I don't think I'm ready to believe that. I'll stick to mapping the enchantments. It will all make sense in the end. Someone certainly thought this place was worth protecting, I just don’t know why. Or how there could be so many convergences of various folklore in one place. And of course you won’t tell me."

"Not everything has to make sense, Eshe. And I don’t know any more than you do. I just embrace the mystery.”

“That’s what studying folklore is all about. I embrace it with love.” Eshe mimed strangling something. “And then when it's guard is down, I throttle the truth out of it.”

Dinah rolled her eyes with a smile. “Good luck pitting yourself against this cottage. I’ve lived here my whole life and I know how stubborn it can be.” She looked around at the walls, the exposed beams, the faded curtains and the much-loved old work surface where her ancestors had baked their own bread for as long as anyone could remember.

“There you go again, saying weird things like that. And then you can’t tell me how you know, or what you mean.”

Dinah shrugged. “I just mean what I mean.” She lifted her head toward the kitchen door, cocking it to one side. She became aware of a change in the air, as if an invisible bubble had appeared outside the cottage, pressing against the walls. She grabbed a tea towel and cleaned her hands heading for the door as she said:

"Mister Hobb's here."

Seconds later a knock came at the door and Eshe raised her palms to the ceiling. "How does she act like that's such a normal thing to be able to do?"

The cottage, as usual, didn't answer. She wasn't sure what she found more annoying; the lack of a response or the fact that she'd started talking to the cottage in the first place. Dinah's eccentricity was rubbing off on her.

Swinging open the wooden front door by its black iron handle, Dinah found Mister Hobb standing a respectful distance from the doorstep. An elderly gentleman with the large nose and ears that come free with advancing age, he wore simple rustic clothing in tweed and rough cotton, and under one arm he carried a wooden tray overflowing with vegetables and bundles of herbs.

"Good morning, Mister Hobb."

He nodded and said only, "Lass."

His attention seemed to be elsewhere, his eye drawn toward the treeline to the south of the cottage.

"How are you today?" she asked, trying to draw anything out of him other than the non-committal snatches he spoke in. She wasn't sure she'd ever heard him speak a full sentence.

Hobb shrugged, still squinting into the distance. In a Yorkshire drawl thicker than Dinah's he said:

"Oh, you know."

She smiled sweetly and nodded. Just as she had expected.

The old man dug in his tray and produced three bundles of herbs, offering them to Dinah with something approaching reverence.

"Thank you so much," she said, receiving only a

nod in return.

Dinah followed his drifting eye to the woods but couldn't see anything in the green haze there. With a gentle push of concentration, she tried to extend her intent that way but found nothing out of the ordinary.

"Something wrong, Mister Hobb?" she asked.

"Nothing," he said. Turning back, he gave her the broad, tight-lipped smile of an old frog. "I'm off."

"Thanks again," Dinah called as the old man turned and left without another word. Herbs in hand, she returned to the kitchen, waving them in the air.

"You'll hate this. I only asked him for this yesterday and he already managed to get it," Dinah said, gesturing to one of the herb bundles with long green stems tipped with tiny red flowers. "Bloodflower. South American."

"And you say he's not a witch?"

Dinah shook her head with a smile. "Not as far as I can tell."

"How can you not ask him how he does it?" Eshe huffed. "I'm going to ask him next time."

Dinah held up a hand. "Nana Haigh always told me it was rude to ask people what they are. Especially around Hexford. It's just another of the wonderful little quirks of the place."

"You said 'what', not 'who'."

Dinah shrugged.

Eshe pointed her finger from the cottage, to Dinah, and then out to where she thought Mister Hobb might be, punctuating each stab by saying: "Weird, weird, weird."

Dinah laughed, took her friend's face in both of her hands, and said, "And you love it."

From her vantage point in the treeline, Isolde Tanner watched Kallin Beck cottage. It didn't look like much as far as she was concerned. The walls were crumbling stone with lopsided lattice windows. There were at least three roofs that she could see, all at different angles to one another, different heights, but all made of the same battered slate dappled with moss. Two chimneys poked at the sky, only one giving off a faint wisp of smoke. Even here Isolde could hear the faint burble of the beck that gave the cottage its name, although it was out of sight at the rear where the dales stretched themselves like a verdant green cat snoozing in the spring sun.

Isolde had followed the old delivery man up the slope from Hexford and positioned herself where, if her spell should fail, she had a decent lead on anyone who might chase her. Just thinking about it, she fiddled with the leather braid on her left wrist from which dangled an unusual charm depicting a single head with three female faces.

As she watched, the Kallin Beck witch answered the door and talked to the old man, Isolde stiffened slightly when he kept looking her way. But she quickly realised there was no need to worry. Her spell worked. They couldn't see her.

The front door to Kallin Beck cottage clicked closed and the old man walked back toward town, having to pass right by Isolde. As he got within touching distance, he looked around, but he still didn't see her. She let a wry smile drift across her cordovan lipstick. The glamour worked even in close quarters.

She shivered. Effective it may be, but the spell

wasn't without its downsides. When she bent the light around her to allow her to become invisible, she also sucked the warmth out of the sunshine. She'd been watching the cottage, waiting for the inhabitants to show themselves for too long and now her fingers were getting numb. She could feel herself growing lethargic as the spell ran on. She needed to go warm up. She really needed a scone and some sugary tea. Then maybe she'd see if she could get inside. There would be wards, of course, and getting over the threshold was going to be the real test of her spell. But that was Future Isolde's problem.

Taking the gentle slope down from Kallin Beck cottage, Isolde headed toward Hexford where she knew a quaint cafe that did the most exquisite scones. Clearing the copse, and certain that no one was watching, she shook her silver-ringed hands, and off fell her glamour. A layer of frost dropped out of the air around her and onto her leather boots and the cuffs of her black jeans. She tugged her similarly black denim jacket tighter over her bell sleeved blouse until she could warm up, and she tucked a strand of her shaggy black bob behind her ear. Wrapping her arms around herself, and hunching her shoulders, Isolde made herself into as small a package as she could as the stony path led her down to the village.

It was an old habit, this physical shrinking when anticipating a crowd. Keeping her elbows tucked in, arms wrapped around her body, Isolde made sure to stay out of anyone's way, to avoid making a nuisance of herself. Not that it was necessary in a place like Hexford. No one ever seemed to give her a second glance. Isolde supposed they saw their fair share of the strange and esoteric to the point that someone like her would barely register on their radar.

Drawing close to the village she saw the mismatched rooftops first; polite little chimneys poking over the hill, nothing with an ambition of being over two storeys high. The main street was a broad avenue of cobbles that ran down the slope, and Hexford was small enough that Isolde could see where the avenue exited the other end of the village from where she had entered. The only thing that truly split the village was a broad stream over glistening rocks with a quaint wooden bridge. People milled around and crossed back and forth pushing wooden wheelbarrows, watering window boxes, or queuing for a single red phone box. It all felt like Isolde could have been in a different time period - depending on which way she was facing at any given moment. Head down and brushing her hair back behind her ear, she made a beeline for the cafe's whitewashed bay window and ducked inside.

CHAPTER TWO

With the fresh scones on their wooden tray covered with a tea towel and balanced on one hand, Dinah clicked the cottage door closed behind her. The leather belt on her oversized cardigan was tied loosely around her waist but she barely needed it. There was a luscious warmth to the morning that soaked in and filled her up.

She couldn't see Eshe, so she pushed out her concentration a little until she could feel the slight fizzing on the roof of her mouth that happened whenever her friend was near. Dinah rounded the house and found the student on her back in the rose bushes.

"Eshe?"

"Don't worry, I'm not dead. I just found a sigil under the basement windowsill that really shouldn't be here."

Dinah bent over to get a better look at where Eshe was peering under the lowest window of the cottage, barely above ground level, and scribbling in what she called a notebook but was in fact a bunch of loose leaves held together with bulldog clips.

"How come?" she asked.

"I thought it was a normal witch mark, but I took a rubbing-" without actually coming out from under the bush, Eshe handed her notebook to Dinah. At the centre of the page was a rubbing of the mark in graphite. "-and it looks like an inscription in cuneiform."

Dinah handed back the book, none the wiser. Eshe often used words she'd never heard as if they were perfectly normal things to say. "The cottage must have wanted you to see it."

Eshe decided not to answer that one but slid out of the bush on her back with branches and dirt all over her shirt and vest. "There's enough here to write a PHD, never mind my Masters."

"Maybe the cottage wants you to stay around."

"Or it's toying with me. Ugh, you've got me doing it as well now."

Dinah just smiled. There was a high probability that it was both. She couldn't deny that since Eshe had arrived on the doorstep asking permission to study the cottage, she'd had a good feeling about her. The offer for the post-grad to stay in the spare room rather than travelling to and from Hexford each day had come easily. And Dinah was certain that the air in the spare room, which should have felt dusty and stale, had been oddly fresh when she'd showed Eshe the way. It was impossible to ignore that Eshe gave off what Dinah's mum would call "good vibes", and that the cottage agreed. However, the old place had a mischievous nature and often showed its affection in odd ways.

"I'm off to work. Try not to lay under the bushes all day. Remember to eat and drink."

Eshe gave a tight-lipped smile as Dinah mothered the younger woman. Then again, Dinah was capable of mothering someone older than her as well.

"Say hi to your Dad for me," was all Eshe said.

Dinah left her friend sitting on the grass, flicking back and forth through her notebook, with an expression of frustration on her face, and headed into town. The gentle slope down to Hexford village was always a pleasant one. The track never felt like it strained her leg muscles, it always allowed gravity to do a little of the work, and no matter the time of year there was a beautiful view of the village rooftops and the dales beyond. Coming up to the village, however, Dinah had to steel herself. From the idyllic isolation of Kallin Beck to the relative hubbub of Hexford caused a leap in what her mother called her "knack" and Eshe called synaesthesia. By the time she reached the High Street, Dinah's mouth was filled with conflicting tastes, her skin twitched and bristled with an indecipherable static of sensations, and auras clashed and morphed before her eyes. She had to focus just to walk down the street without wafting away or shouting over sensations that were invisible to others.

Luckily, the closer a source was, the stronger it became, and as Dinah's friend Charlie stepped toward her, the smell of fresh sawdust that came with his proximity washed everything else away. She never knew how the sensations were attributed to people, but she thought Charlie's might have been from the almost white blond hair and eyebrows that made her think of a hamster.

"You don't think that you can just carry those scones through town without being accosted, do you?" Charlie asked, lifting the corner of the tea towel to peer beneath.

Dinah slapped his hand. "Oy. These are for The Nook."

"Meredith won't miss one."

"She will and you know it. Get your mitts off."

With an exaggerated sigh, Charlie gave up. "I'm glad I've caught you. I needed to ask you about something."

Dinah stayed quiet to let her friend continue and in the space of the silence Charlie became a little too still for her liking, apart from his eyes which were drawn away from Dinah as he spoke.

"Do you have anything for nightmares?" Charlie asked.

"Have something? Not really."

"No, I know you don't do that kind of thing. But I've been having these weird dreams lately and they're keeping me up at night."

Dinah finally noticed that Charlie, usually quite fresh faced, was looking a little grey.

"It could be anxiety," Dinah offered. "Are you stressed out?"

Charlie laughed but his heart clearly wasn't in it. "Running the library is hardly stressful around here. I don't think we've had a single late book or copy out of place as long as I've been here."

"Something else, then?" asked Dinah, and without wanting to push she added, "Everything ok at home?"

"Yeah, yeah. Everything's fine. Theo's grand. I know not everything's—" Charlie wiggled his fingers in a way that he thought conveyed magic. "But these dreams. Dinah, I wake up petrified enough that I can't close my eyes again."

That was enough to pique Dinah's interest a little more - even if she didn't have Charlie down as the precognitive type, it was best to be careful. "What do you see?"

"That's the thing. Not a clue. It feels like- like I'm halfway to death before I get snatched back. It's driving Theo nuts."

With a hand on Charlie's arm, Dinah pushed out a little concentration through her fingers, trying to glean any sensation at all from her friend. "I don't feel anything wrong with you, Charlie. Nothing—" she wiggled her fingers with a faint smile. "But let me look into it when I get home, ok? I'm sure one of Mum's books will have something that can help."

Charlie didn't seem as reassured as she had hoped, even when he quipped, "Yeah. Yeah, thanks. You best get those scones where they're going before I snatch one, eh? And come for tea soon?"

Dinah squeezed his arm a little before letting go. "That sounds lovely. I'll let you know the second I find something."

Moving on, and with the storm of stimuli returning, she took a glance back at Charlie who lingered on the spot for a second before walking off. She hoped that there would be something in her mother's books to help Charlie sleep, but she knew she'd have to be careful. Her nan, and then her mum after her, were real witches with real power. They knew about tonics and elixirs, spells and enchantments and all that stuff, but Dinah wasn't that kind of witch. Sure, she put a little magic into her baking to make it extra scrumptious and filled with little benefits to anyone who ate it, but that was as far as she went. If Charlie needed a real witch's help, he was barking up the wrong tree. Still, as much as that was true, everyone she passed on her way gave her a nod, a smile, a knowing wink. Everyone saw the Witch of Kallin Beck where Dinah saw Just Dinah. The threat of disappointing the entire town was ever present.

The bakery was a long and low building on Hexford Main Street, made from uneven stones that fit like puzzle pieces, with dusty mortar between them. The door didn't have a lock, just an old iron latch, but there was a witch's mark on the door frame; an Auseklis Cross with added snowflake fronds that was her mother's personal mark. Dinah tapped it twice with her fingertip for good luck, and stepped inside.

The bakery was two steps down from the street. Dinah's boots clacked on the time-smoothed flagstones as she approached the long, wooden counter that ran in an L-shape across the middle of the room. The counter's slanted boxes were already filled with loaves and buns, stout stotties and long baguettes, flour coated or seed-studded. Dinah closed her eyes, feeling the flood of sensations from the street outside peel away to be replaced with only the smell of bread and the almost uncomfortable warmth exuding from the kitchen to the rear. This was the closest to bliss she could be without being in her own kitchen.

"I'll just be a minute!" came a voice from the kitchen.

"It's me, Dad," Dinah called back.

"Ooh!" came the excited reply. "Do you have the scones?"

Dinah smiled to herself and made for the kitchen.

Apart from the large grey moustache and rolled shirt sleeves rather than a cardigan, Gabe Nye was the spitting image of his daughter. When he saw Dinah, and the tray she was carrying, he dusted the flour from his hands and came scooting over with glee. He peeked under the tea towel, regarded Dinah with a glint in his eye, and then hugged her as warmly as he could with only one arm so that his floury apron didn't press against her.

"I can already tell they're scrumptious," he said. He was almost dancing on the flagstones with excitement.

"Well, number thirteen is for you."

"Put the kettle on and I'll slather it in butter. We can go halves."

With time-earned efficiency they moved around each other in the bakery, retrieving sugar and milk, butter and jam. When they sat on the high stools next to Gabe's bench, he made what Dinah thought of as an 'old man noise'.

"You ok, Dad?" she asked.

"Just old, love."

She smiled but it ran cold through her. It was hard to think of her father as an old man. Sure, his hair and moustache were grey, and his laughter lines were multiplying. But the way he had of skipping around the bakery, grinning as he tore the scone into halves, and poking out his tongue when slathering them with butter and jam, Dinah could always see more of a happy baking boy in him than an old man.

Taking a bite of Dinah's scone, he caught butter and jam in his moustache.

"If I could bake like this, I'd die happy," he said, spitting crumbs.

"Good job you can't, then. Because you're not going anywhere."

Dinah picked up her own half and took a big bite. She had to admit, all modesty aside, that this batch was pretty darned good.

"Have you heard from Mum?" she asked.

"Nope. And we're not likely to. She'll have her head against a tree somewhere, her mind in the branches and leaves," he said with a chuckle. "Trees don't use telephones. Neither do rocks or streams or—" he gestured with both hands to encompass everything.

"What do you really think she'll find?"

Wiping his hand down his moustache and then his hand on his floury apron, Gabe's face was sweet but sad.

"Between you and me? I'm not hopeful, love. But she has to try."

"You think the beck's been quiet too long, don't you?"

"I think that whatever gave it its magic has moved on. Me and your Mum spent years on those banks, chatting to the water and the sky, at midday and midnight, and we never heard a whisper. You know that's where you were—"

Dinah threw up a hand. "Please don't."

Gabe chuckled and took another bite of his scone.

"Made with love, you were. That's all I'm saying."

"And with that—" Dinah said, dusting her hands, which was both her and Gabe's way of signalling the end of anything from a good job to an uncomfortable conversation. "Meredith will be wanting the rest of the batch. Do you have anything for her?"

Cramming the last of his scone into his mouth and slurping tea through the crumbs, Gabe collected a larger wooden tray already laden with breads and cakes, put Dinah's scones on top, and handed it over.

"Thank you, love," he said. "Say hello to Mer for me."

Taking the tray, Dinah kissed her father on the cheek. "You have a good day."

"Always!" he called after her as the bakery door clicked closed.

Steering the large tray through Hexford was surprisingly easy. Anyone who spotted Dinah, spotted the tray, knew what was in it, knew the taste and joy of the goods inside, and so respectfully stepped aside to let her through with a knowing wink or tip of a cap.

The Nook, Hexford's only cafe, wasn't far. Soon Dinah was reversing through its barn-style door. But rather than a straw-strewn floor and animal smells, the inside was toasty warm and chintzy.

"Life saver!" Although the cafe was bustling, no one reacted to Meredith's outburst as Dinah waddled in. They were all well used to the owner's demeanour matching her bustling establishment.

Meredith came out from behind the counter in a half apron, wiping her hands and throwing the towel over her shoulder. Her curly brunette hair was pulled back into a scrunchy straining with the effort of holding in the explosion of dark springs. As she came closer, Dinah's knack gave her the sensation of slipping on a pair of coarse wool gloves.

"Dinah, tell me those are fresh scones."

"These are fresh scones," Dinah said, offering the tray to Meredith who sniffed the air over the tray. "And bread buns, a few loaves, the lot."

"I say again: lifesaver. I just sold my last one."

Meredith gave a vague wave toward a young woman sitting at the back of the cafe, in the nook that gave the place its name, as she led Dinah through to the kitchen. Hunched at the shoulders and slid slightly down in her seat, the dark-haired and pale young woman was holding a large mug as if she might throw the contents on someone if they approached - but Dinah wasn't sure if it would be out of spite or fright. Despite herself, she pushed her concentration toward the stranger but there were too many people in The Nook, too many sensations for her knack to separate out a single one.

The young woman's head snapped up and their eyes locked for a fleeting moment. Dinah knew a witch when she sensed one, so she gave the girl a smile. The witch flicked her eyes back to the tabletop in front of her, tucked her black hair behind her ear, and that seemed to be that. Dinah ducked into the kitchen without a second thought. Some witches preferred to practice alone, and this young woman seemed to be one of them.

"These are still a little bit warm," Meredith cooed.

"You're lucky they're all there. Charlie nearly snatched one on my way over."

"Wait til I see him. Are we ok to keep going with

the standard order? And I'll pay you end of the month, I promise."

Dinah waved a hand and said, "Don't fret. Just let me know if you run out again."

"Tea?"

"Tea."

While Dinah sat in the cafe's kitchen drinking her tea, Meredith continued to work, chatting the whole time and sometimes switching between three tracks of thought. Only once did she stop for a second, her back to the kitchen wall and her head back, taking a breather. Dinah eyed her.

"You alright?"

"Yeah, yeah. Just knackered," Meredith said. "Nothing unusual." Dinah stayed quiet, just raising her eyebrows at her friend until she continued. "I've just not been sleeping right."

Dinah paused with her teacup halfway to her mouth, waiting for what came next and hoping that it wouldn't be what she suspected.

"Been having these horrible flaming nightmares. Stress from running this place, probably."

"Tell me everything you can remember," Dinah said, with such seriousness that Meredith stuttered a little.

"It's- I don't really remember them."

"But they're scary? Enough to stop you sleeping?"

"Yeah, I suppose."

Dinah set down her cup. "You're the second person today."

"Oh." Meredith actually sat down on the stool opposite Dinah, something she'd never seen her do before. "What do you think it is?"

"Maybe nothing."

"But maybe something."

"I'll have a look just in case. Probably everyone is eating too much cheese before bed," Dinah said with a smile she hoped was comforting. Meredith didn't seem convinced for a second.

"Better get off."

"Yeah, course."

On her way out, Dinah nearly collided with the young witch dressed all in black. "Oh, sorry."

"Umm, sorry," the young witch said, barely audible.

"You first."

"No, it's ok."

Sensing a politeness stand-off and now really wanting to get home, Dinah smiled swiftly and scootched out of the door, heading off up the High Street toward Kallin Beck with enough intent that she barely felt the town around her.

Back in The Nook, Meredith asked the young witch, "You alright, love? Another cuppa?"

"No. Thank you. I shouldn't have come," Isolde said as she ducked out as well.

Chapter Three

"What are you hiding, house?" Eshe said with her mouth full of ham sandwich. From her vantage point on the bank of the beck, her bare feet splashing in the ever-clear water that ran between banks of mossy earth, she eyed the lopsided old place. It looked smug, she decided.

This was supposed to be an easy assignment. In the right circles, Kallin Beck was underground famous for being the witchiest place in England. But Eshe hadn't been able to find a single academic article about the place. So, she'd decided she would just have to go and check the place out, write her dissertation on how cool it was, and pass with flying colours. And it had been an excuse to come and see it. But now that she was here, she could almost understand why there was nothing written about it. She imagined that anyone who came, took one look, realised that the gordian knot of magical signs and sigils were historically indecipherable, and then went home again, never to mention the fact that they'd failed.

"But you've never met Eshe Morgan, House," she said, pointing her sandwich at the old cottage and then waving it in a wide circle. "I'm your match."

Taking a long swig from a bottle of apple juice, she took up her current notebook. She'd made several rubbings of the apotropaic marks which were secreted on every surface, threshold, and material of the cottage. Crosshatches, interconnected triangles and circles, knots and letters filled the pages. Of course, the marks were little metaphors for protection; stories told in their simplest form, in which a world could be held at bay by the correct sweep of charcoal or shape of a carving in wood. And the women who had lived in Kallin Beck cottage had needed protection more than most, it seemed. That's what fascinated Eshe, really, the origins of the diagrams, cyphers, and carvings, and why the women of this cottage, in this place, had felt that they needed so many from all over the world. How badly persecuted had they been?

Removing one bulldog clip that held her notebook closed, as opposed to the others which served as binding, she rifled through the pages of annotated rubbings and sketches. It seemed that over the centuries since it had been built, the cottage had been home to many generations of witches and been visited by maybe hundreds more, just as Dinah had told her. In fact, the place was so old that there were no surviving records showing when the cottage had actually been built. Eshe had to admit that as fascinated with the folklore - and as eager to complete her Masters as she was, the thought of being able to reunite Dinah and her family with a piece of their lost lineage was pretty compelling as well. At the very least, it would be a nice thing to do for someone who had let Eshe stay with her for months without ever asking for anything in return.

All she had to do was make a note of the origins of the apotropaic marks used around the cottage, map their origins, both in time and geographically, and figure out how they could possibly have ended up in the middle of the Yorkshire dales.

So, incredibly difficult, then.

"I'll figure you out eventually," Eshe said to the house. "But first, I'm going to stop talking to you. Because even Dinah doesn't do that."

Eshe was packing up her simple lunch when Dinah came around the cottage. For a moment, they were on opposite banks of the Kallin Beck with the sweet, clear water running between them.

"You're home early," Eshe said, brushing off her trousers.

"I had to tell Dad I was needed at home. There's something going on," Dinah replied. "Something in town."

Eshe faltered over the final word when she said, "You mean something magical?"

"Maybe. I could use your help." Dinah said, holding out her hand to her friend over the beck. Eshe used the largest rocks to hop over the stream and, still holding her hand, Dinah led her back to the cottage.

In the kitchen, Dinah paused at a small bookcase filled with cookery books to grab a leather-bound tome unlike the others, before leading Eshe through to the dining room. With the single book still conspicuously tucked under her arm, Dinah gestured to the dining room bookcase filled with more books.

"Ok, you start up there, I'll start in here," she said, waving her book.

"And we're looking for…?"

"Anything about bad dreams," Dinah said distractedly as she took a seat at the dining table and began to leaf through the book.

Eshe watched her friend for a second. The only time she'd seen Dinah focus this hard was when she was making bread dough. Taking down a book at random, she took a seat and began to read.

"No. Nothing. There's just stupid recipes in here." Dinah gripped the sides of her recipe book so tight that her fingers paled. Eshe thought she might throw it across the room but instead she put it down with a slap. "What kind of witch has a Book of Shadows with no useful information in it?"

Eshe eyed her. "That's your Book of Shadows?"

"It's supposed to be. But it's all teacakes and herbal brews." Dinah put her face in her hands and screamed through them. "I'm the worst witch Hexford's ever seen."

"Hey," Eshe said, rounding the table to kneel beside her friend. "What's going on with you, Dinah?"

With her hands still covering her face , Dinah mumbled. "Nothing. I just don't know any of this stuff. Mum tried to teach me, and I never could take it in. Now two of my friends are having these weird nightmares and I think it's something magical, but I can't help them because all I can do is bake and make tea."

"Ok, well let's start there, then," Eshe said. "Go put the kettle on and we'll start this again. Properly and together."

Dinah sniffed, but dragged herself off to the kitchen to take a breath and make some tea. By the time she came back with two steaming mugs of tea, Eshe had retrieved her paper, pens, and more books.

"Feel better?" Eshe asked.

Dinah nodded.

"I know how you feel, you know," Eshe said. "My first year of uni, I was exactly the same. Everyone in my class were all from upper class places that taught kids Chaucer when they were five. I was just this girl from an inner-city school where you were lucky to get the books you needed. I felt really out of my depth, like everyone was miles ahead of me. But I had one thing they didn't."

"What was it?" Dinah asked.

Eshe gestured to an A3 notepad and a pencil case on the table. "I was organised."

Sitting across from each other, cups of tea nearby, Eshe ripped a page from the notepad and grabbed a marker pen.

"Right, let's start with what we're after." In the middle of the page, she wrote, 'bad dreams', circled it, and drew a line from the circle. "What do we know about magic and dreams?"

"Fairies can send you dreams?" Dinah said.

Eshe wrote, 'fairies', at the end of the first line, circled it, and then drew another line. "What else? Omens and portents. They're all over ancient myths. Everyone and their dog gets a premonition dream at some point."

"I hope it's not important because they can't remember anything from the dream."

"Right, let's make a side list. I'll start with 'bad dreams', then 'can't remember'. This will help us narrow things down."

"Add to it that they can't sleep afterward. Oh, and that they felt really scared when they woke up."

And so, slowly, they worked on the problem. Soon they had a map of possibilities, half-remembered stories and titbits spread across the page.

"And now to the books. But we have a framework to work from, you see?" Eshe said.

"I don't know how you do that so easily," Dinah said.

"Practice," Eshe said. "Same as you know how to bake any number of things without even looking at a recipe and pour so much love into it that people scream for more. I wouldn't have a clu—"

Eshe came up short as Dinah's arms wrapped around her shoulders from behind in a weird reverse hug that clumsily encompassed the chair back as well.

"Thank you, Eshe."

Eshe patted Dinah's hand as it was the only part she could reach. "Let's get reading, shall we?"

Mugs of tea were drunk, replaced, and drunk again. The sun began to go down over the dales and the big light was clicked on. Hot bowls of yesterday's soup with huge chunks of soft, buttered bread were devoured, and still the friends kept reading. Curses, hexes, hauntings and creatures were bandied back and forth but it all amounted to the same thing: they knew too little to narrow it all down.

"We should get some sleep," Eshe said eventually. "Tired brain make no read good."

Dinah groaned. "But Charlie and Meredith could be out there having more terrible nightmares while I'm tucked up in bed."

"We can't help them if we're exhausted too." Eshe rubbed her eyes and closed her book. "Or we could just go with the succubus idea."

"You want it to be a succubus," Dinah said with a chuckle.

"Come on, Dinah. It'd be spicaaay!"

They both laughed but it petered out into tired sighs.

"You're right, we should sleep," Dinah admitted, and she started to get up from the table. "We can start again tomorrow."

"Dinah."

Dinah looked up at Eshe, who was wearing a very careful expression of concern.

"Yes?"

"Be honest with me. Do you really believe in all this stuff?" Eshe asked conspiratorially. "There's only you and me here. No tricks, no half answers. I'm sure you've been brought up with it your whole life. We all have families that indoctrinate us into their cultures, their beliefs. My family are all ardent Christian church-goers, so I know that it's important to your family that Kallin Beck is a special place. And you know that I love this folklore stuff. It's fascinating. But as my friend, tell me honestly. Do you really believe this stuff?"

Dinah gave her a tired smile. "I don't need to believe. I certainly don't need to know." Her brow knotted as she tried to find the words. "One day your mind just opens up to possibility, and you're left with this fantastic sense of 'maybe'. And that maybe holds in its hands the souls in trees and invisible particles, things that are weighed in thought and that only exist if you catch a glimpse of them. You know?"

Eshe shook her head with a smile.

Dinah chuckled. "Let's go to bed."

Chapter Four

Stupid, stupid, Isolde. You spend weeks of work to be invisible and then you're spotted right out in the open.

If her mother found out, Isolde would be in deep trouble. As it was, maybe she could pull it back. The Kallin Beck witch hadn't seemed to give her a second glance even when she'd spotted Isolde and they had recognised each other as practitioners. If Isolde could just keep her head down and get access to the cottage tonight, then all would be well. But something was itching at her, something that her mother had glossed over.

Isolde's mother, Amabel, was the head of the Tanner family coven, which consisted of Isolde's younger sister, Vivian, and older sister, Lucia, conspicuously skipping over Isolde in the middle.

Isolde was left with the task of runner, which meant that she was often away from home investigating something or someone, or left to do vital research which the coven had no time for. Isolde usually considered the work to be a series of never-ending inanities, but this time her mother had entrusted her with a task of real importance: spy on the Kallin Beck witch. When she had asked, Isolde had been given flimsy reasoning. The cottage was a site of great significance to the supernatural community of England and should be surveyed. But that didn't sit quite right with Isolde. If it was of such importance, and there were only fellow witches inside, then why not just knock on the door and introduce herself? No, Mother had something else up her sleeve and she didn't trust Isolde enough to share it.

As she stepped out of The Nook, arms still wrapped around her, Isolde wondered what it was that could have her mother so interested in the old cottage. The village of Hexford itself was of far more interest, as far as she could see. Although it looked like a normal place, Isolde could sense the tingle of enchantment in the air wherever she went. Hexford was blessed - the whole town - and the enchantment was so subtle, so clever, that no one seemed to be aware of it. Ducking into a side street, Isolde bounced in her steps a little as if testing gravity, receiving little sparks of magical feedback through her boots each time. The enchantment was similar to her own invisibility spell in the way that it was a nudge rather than a push, a gentle request to Nature to look favourably on the village.

Isolde found herself smiling a little at the cleverness of it. Winters were crisp, Autumns balmy, in Summer there was always a blissful breeze, and Spring came easily when it was due. Someone had put a lot of work into making Hexford a fine place to be, and that extended to making sure that it slipped from any mapmaker's mind as well. With time to kill until her evening's spying, Isolde thought she would spend some time in the local library and try to find out more about the place.

The building itself was an innocuous stone rectangle with a painted lintel above the door embossed with the word 'library'. The windows were arched, panes leaded, and there were posters advertising groups and activities taped into each one. As Isolde stepped inside, a blast of warm air from the heater over the door was almost overpowering and she rushed through it, finding herself in the silent space before she was really ready. As she expected, it was empty. She couldn't see the librarian or any other patrons but she supposed they could be hidden somewhere between the large oak bookshelves and modern-looking rotundas. This actually played into her comfort zone and so she started to quietly browse. Everything seemed to be pretty normal. The fiction section was full of slightly outdated thrillers and romances, the children's section was strewn with a mix of toys and books in primary colours, and study tables in the middle of the space had little home-made pots of pens and pencils free to use. But there didn't seem to be anything about local history which Isolde found suspicious.

"Hiya."

Isolde spun around, her fingers engaged into an eldritch configuration of protection crackling with warding energy, a word of power hanging on her lips.

Charlie stood in front of her in his home-knitted sweater, arms full of books, eyebrows as high as they would go. "Blimey."

Isolde dropped her hands instantly, stuffing them into her jacket pockets. "Sorry."

"Didn't mean to startle you, miss. But in a place like this, anything other than silence sounds like a gunshot, you know?"

"Yes, of course," Isolde said. "Sorry."

"You can let the spell fizzle if you want. It must be hurting your fingers holding it like that," Charlie said, dropping the books onto his desk.

Slowly, Isolde withdrew her hands and shook out the magic, which was starting to smart, actually.

Charlie kept on chattering as if he'd been storing it up for days. "We don't get many practitioners in here, to be fair. They usually like to keep their own books, you know?"

"I was looking for something about local history," Isolde offered, still slightly confused by the librarian's nonchalance. Was Hexford really so used to the supernatural? Everywhere she'd ever been the occult and esoteric practices were under the table, off the beaten track, or straight-up denied entirely.

"New to the area, then? I didn't think I'd seen you around. You'll like it here."

"I'm not staying."

Charlie kinked an eyebrow. "Right. Well, just the research then? The old stuff is in the back. I'll show you."

Isolde trailed behind the librarian through a rear door into a tightly shelved area filled with labelled cardboard boxes and box files. At the back of the room, in a well-lit corner, was an old computer and even older microfiche reader.

"It's exactly as clunky as it looks," Charlie offered. "Have you used one before?"

Isolde nodded.

"I'll get out of your way, then. Usual caveat: please put things back where you find them. We're open all day so no rush."

The librarian disappeared back out of the archive, leaving Isolde alone.

Newspapers, council meeting minutes, obituaries, and more cycled before Isolde's eyes for the next few hours. All of it maddeningly boring. There seemed to be absolutely nothing obscure or fascinating about Hexford, other than that she knew for a fact that it was enchanted from boundary to boundary and had a famous witch's cottage on the edge. Pulling away from the microfiche to rest her eyes for a second, Isolde pondered the anomaly in tandem with the librarian's laissez faire attitude to magic. She could think of only one explanation: the villagers saw the supernatural as so fundamental to their way of life that magical happenings were no longer worth reporting on. But she couldn't accept that.

Exiting the archive, Isolde hadn't realised how weirdly angry she'd gotten with the conundrum until she shoved the door a little too hard and it slammed into the wall behind it.

Charlie, who had been mid-yawn, nearly fell off his chair.

"There's nothing in there," Isolde said. "Where's all the magic? The incursions and monsters, the-danger."

"Nothing like that here, miss," said Charlie,

seeming absolutely genuine. "Hexford's not like that. Magic's like- the milk being delivered. It just happens, you know? And we're grateful for it. If we have any problems, we have the Kallin Beck witch. I've not been sleeping right, for instance, so she's looking into something to help."

"That's not what a witch is, that's a chemist," Isolde said, throwing her hands up.

Charlie chuckled. "Well, we have one of those as well. Have a seat, I'll put the kettle on."

Despite herself, Isolde flopped down at a table. This was entirely contrary to anything she'd ever known about magic. Magic was loose, dangerous, a force to be harnessed with focus and diligence. It was the craft in witchcraft, the practice in practitioner. And from that came great power, honour, and wisdom. These Hexford witches were agony aunts and charm peddlers. And that's when it hit her. Her mother's motivation. Somewhere like Kallin Beck cottage, with such lineage, fame, and presumably power, should be under the guidance of a coven, not a baker of especially good scones.

This assignment really was important to her mother. She was planning on the Tanner coven taking over Kallin Beck.

Charlie backed out of the kitchen with a tea tray, the teapot sloshing a little.

"Might want to give it a minute to stew," he said, turning around and realising that he was talking to himself. The young witch had gone.

Chapter Five

The alarm was loud enough to rattle the windows of Kallin Beck. Eshe felt like it had rattled her right out of bed like a Tom and Jerry cartoon. She burst out onto the landing, still in her sleep cap and bare footed, dragging on her dressing gown, and nearly collided with Dinah hurtling out of her own room opposite. Dinah brandished an iron poker like a baseball bat, her dressing gown flapping open and her hair loose. She'd taken a second to tug on her outdoor boots, but the laces trailed.

"I take it that isn't the fire alarm," Eshe shouted over the ear-shredding sound.

Dinah shook her head and yelled back, "Something's trying to get into the cottage."

"Some—" Dinah stalked away toward the stairs, poker held ready to swing. Eshe thought fast, ducked back into her room for a weapon, and came out holding her vintage hair dryer in one hand, the plug end in the other.

Checking back for her friend before taking the first step down, Dinah eyed the hairdryer and tightened her lips to hide her smile. It didn't work.

"Not all of us sleep with weapons by our beds," Eshe yelled.

Step by step, Dinah bent double to scan the lower floor as much as possible as they crept down to the ground floor. Eshe hopped from one foot to the other on the freezing flagstones.

As they reached the hallway, the alarm snapped off - which was somehow worse. Straining to listen and scanning every corner, they both waited for their ears to stop ringing, waited for something to show itself, waited to defend the cottage with their improvised weapons.

"I didn't know you had a burglar alarm," Eshe whispered.

"I don't."

Eshe didn't bother to comment on her lack of surprise.

Dinah's eyes did that thing where they lost focus and Eshe realised that her friend was using her knack, pushing out her concentration in an effort to sense something.

"What is it?"

"I'm not getting anything," Dinah said, creeping closer to the door.

"Careful, Dinah."

"Don't worry. It'd take something really special to

get through the wards. I just want to get a hint of it, something that might help find it."

Eshe's hand landed lightly on Dinah's shoulder as she followed her friend forward. "You think it's the thing that's after Meredith and Charlie?"

"Maybe. It might just be a lost spirit bumping into the cottage. But I'm still not feeling anything." She twitched aside the curtain on the little window beside the door. "Can't see anything either. I think it's gone."

"Oh, thank God," Eshe said, letting her hairdryer drop to her side.

Dinah lowered her poker, but she still seemed pensive.

"What's wrong?" Eshe asked.

"If it is the thing we're looking for, and it can't get in here, it'll likely go find someone else," Dinah replied. "Maybe I should follow it."

"That'd be mental. What are you going to do in the dark, half-cocked and in your jimjams?"

Dinah mulled that over. "Yeah. Good point. I'll find it tomorrow."

"We both will."

Dinah smiled sadly. "Thanks. Let's get back to bed. I think tomorrow's going to be a long day."

"Like I'll sleep now."

"I have just the thing. Hot milk with vanilla and nutmeg. It'll put you right out." Dinah led the way toward the kitchen, but stopped so sharply that Eshe bumped into her back. Snapping her head back toward the door, Dinah licked her lips.

"What is it?" Eshe asked, looking at the door even though she didn't expect to see anything.

It was faint, but Dinah thought she tasted:

"Liquorice."

Her back against the shady side of the low stone wall around Kallin Beck's garden, Isolde rubbed her aching body. The wards hadn't just pushed back, they had knocked her flying. Her skin itched all over as if she'd rolled in poison ivy. She had expected a little resistance, of course, but not this. She had relatively benign intent, after all, only wanting to peek inside, not hurt anyone. The cottage's wards had reacted like she'd brought an army. If it did that every time a curious fox or hungry hedgehog got near, she was amazed that the area around it wasn't a scorched wasteland. Her mother was right, this place was dangerous and needed to be studied.

Taking a peek over the wall, Isolde saw a curtain twitch and she ducked again. She was ready to run into the woods if need be, but she hoped that they wouldn't chase her because she couldn't make herself invisible again just yet. It was as if the wards had grounded her, sucking all her power out through her feet. Damn the place.

Straining her ears, she didn't hear any click of locks, or footsteps in the garden. They were staying inside. And why wouldn't they, with a magical fortress to hide in. After a while, when she was sure that there would be no pursuit, Isolde slinked off back to her campsite. The worst part of her night, the itching, gradually subsided and back came the sensation of power, starting in her toes and working upward. Not that a midnight stroll through a forest worried her in the slightest even without her magic. She was confident that she was the thing that other people wouldn't want to come across in the dark.

The night was blissfully cool until she stepped out beyond Hexford's boundary and the true temperature snapped in. Even though the spring temperatures were pleasant during the day, the night retained the sharp edges of winter. Perhaps it would have been wise to have made her camp just a little closer to town to take advantage of the Hexford enchantment. But that felt a little like she might have been sleeping in enemy territory - at least until she knew more about the place.

Isolde came across her first athame stuck in the ground and waved a hand over it as she walked by. The steel knife with its simple crossguard was one of three that she used for many purposes. Right now, they were marking a warding circle around her own camp. Although, unlike the Kallin Beck cottage, Isolde's spell merely suggested to anyone who approached that they should turn aside and take a circuitous route around the area, or that they had taken a wrong turn somewhere back along their way. Subtle and clever, just how Isolde liked her spells.

The camp, consisting of Isolde's small dome tent and a cleared area of earth that she had been using for spellwork and her camping stove, appeared untouched. It wasn't much, but it was home. Crawling into her tent, Isolde zipped up the door and put a little magic into the frame. The chill dropped out of the air. It would get cold again as she slept, she knew, but it would be enough to help her drop off. Taking off her coat, she stayed clothed and crawled into her sleeping bag. From the hiking pack beside her she took an oaty protein bar and gnawed at it.

She gave a little chuckle as something rose to her mind, the image of her, a Tanner witch, curled up like a dormouse. She doubted the rest of her family would be cold tonight, or that they'd wake up with a rock in their back or a crick in their neck. Her mother would have her long black nightgown covering her from chin to toes and be lying down as if she was practising for an open casket. Lucia would have fallen asleep between the voile curtains of her four-poster bed with a book on her chest. And Vivian? She would likely be awake all the way to morning.

Isolde tried to put her youngest sister out of her mind. It would only upset her before she settled down. No, better to think of Kallin Beck and how she was going to get in there to poke around. There had to be a way. If she thought about it right up until sleep, perhaps she'd dream the answer.

Chapter Six

"That's not a good sign," Dinah said under her breath.

She and Eshe stared at a 'closed' sign dangling from the door of The Nook. People came, saw the sign, and left crestfallen. The Nook provided most of Hexford with food or coffee at some point in the day. Not to mention Dinah's Home-from-home Scones.

"There's going to be a lot of hungry, cranky people," Eshe said.

"Let's hope that's as bad as it gets," Dinah replied, heading off down a side street with her friend in tow.

Eshe had noticed that Dinah was always quiet when they came into town, almost brusque. But this morning she was especially terse. The worry, perhaps, was getting to her.

"Should we check on Meredith?" she asked.

"We will. But we need to try the library first."

Approaching the old stone building, they could already see from a distance that the closed sign still hung on the library door as well. Neither of them said a word, they just walked right on by with Dinah leading the way.

"Meredith then Charlie," Dinah muttered in answer to what neither of them were saying aloud. "She lives alone."

"Oh God, Dinah. What if something's happened to her?"

Dinah took what felt like an age to reply. "I don't know."

Heading toward the cafe owner's home, Dinah wanted to run so badly that she could feel her leg muscles straining, but she forced herself to a mere brisk walk. If she ran, her rising panic would get a hold of her, and she wasn't sure she could make it let go again.

The front of Meredith's house was only one door and a window wide, and just one home in a row of tall, narrow terraced houses that led down a cobbled hill. Dinah knocked on the door and the lack of an answer strung out into an uncomfortable silence.

Eshe had her nose to the single window, peeking through a gap in the curtains. She tapped Dinah on the shoulder and moved aside so she could see in. Through the gap, Dinah could see a sliver of Meredith's living room, which was just as chintzy as The Nook, and through the kitchen door to a small table. There sat Meredith in her pyjamas and slippers, her head resting on the table, using her folded arms as a pillow.

"You don't think she's—" Eshe started to say, but Dinah interrupted her by banging on the little window with the flat of her hand.

Inside, Meredith shot upright, her eyes bleary and her body swaying even before she tried to stand. But stand she did, and she slowly made her way to open the front door. Dinah could hear her scraping the old iron key against the door, as if she didn't have enough coordination to fit it into the lock.

"Dinah? Are you alright?" Meredith asked as the door swung open.

"Well, I can put a hold on my heart attack at least," Dinah said.

"Eh?"

"It's nine o'clock, Mer."

"Oh no!" Meredith looked for a second like she was going to bolt back into the house, grab her shoes, and run out of the door to open up The Nook, which she usually had open by seven. But her body just wouldn't let her. She sagged instead, and Dinah had to step inside to take her arm. As Eshe closed the door and kicked off her shoes, Dinah plonked their stricken friend down in the living room.

"I just need a minute," Meredith muttered.

Dinah searched her ashen face. "More bad dreams?"

"Mhm."

"I'll put the kettle on," Eshe suggested, with little else to offer.

With a hand on Meredith's, Dinah talked in a low voice. "Do you remember what you dreamed about, Mer? Anything at all."

"No. I'm just so tired," Meredith muttered. "If I

could go back to sleep right now, I'd sleep forever."

Eshe stood in the doorway and her eyes met Dinah's. Sure, it was an innocuous thing to say. They'd said it, or something like it, themselves. But a shudder ran through them nonetheless.

"I'll stay with Meredith," Eshe said. "You better go check on Charlie."

Charlie's place was on the same street, lower down the cobbled hill. His house was the same layout and, as it turned out, easier to gain access to. As Dinah banged on the door hard enough to make her hand sting, it swung open as if it had been waiting for her.

"Am I ever glad to see you."

Charlie's husband Theo was shorter than the librarian, dark haired, with large dark eyes and eyelashes that made Dinah envious. He was usually well turned out, even on his days off or while slobbing around the house, but he answered the door still in his rumpled pyjamas with a bobbled old hoodie over the top. Dinah's knack gave her the taste of her grandmother's custard, a pleasant, creamy vanilla.

Theo walked back into the house and Dinah followed him up the stairs without ceremony.

"Charlie's still in bed. I can't get him up at all. He said he'd talked to you. Do you think he's ill? Should I call a doctor or is it—"

Dinah put a hand on Theo's shoulder just before they stepped into the bedroom.

"Honestly? I don't know. But there's something going round. It might be just a dose of the flu, you know?"

"I've never known the flu to have you screaming and clawing at the walls at night," Theo said. His voice was trembling. Seeing him shaken was contagious and Dinah felt the urge to walk away without opening the bedroom door at all.

"He didn't say it was so bad," she said.

Theo shook his head. "Last night was the worst. First, he's too afraid to close his eyes and now he's so tired. You'll see."

Leading the way, Theo pushed into the bedroom. There was Charlie, lying on his back with the covers pulled up under his chin. He was snoring, his face grey just like Meredith's. Dinah approached and touched his clammy forehead, but Charlie didn't even flinch.

"He's out cold," offered Theo, his arms folded tight around him. "I can get him to wake up for a few seconds if I really shout and shake him, but that's it."

"Let's let him rest," Dinah said.

"I don't think he's getting any, even when he does sleep. He's exhausted."

Dinah shook her head. "I'm so sorry, Theo. I'm going to fix this."

I just don't know how, she added to herself.

"Do you mind if I poke around a bit?"

Theo gave a vague wave of the hand and Dinah set to work. She checked the window frame and sill, under the bed, the standing mirror in the corner of the room and under the rug. There were no obvious signs, sigils, hex bags, or anything else she recognised that might allow a creature access to the house, or that could have been used as a conduit for magic.

"Have you talked to Sarah yet?" Theo asked as Dinah poked around.

Dinah shook her head. "I don't think I know her."

"The bus driver? Short blonde hair." Theo tapped

his eyebrow. "Piercing here?"

"I've seen her around, I think. I don't use the bus much. I don't go anywhere but here," Dinah said, peeking behind an abstract painting hanging opposite the bed.

"I saw her yesterday. Grey, tired. Said she'd not been sleeping," Theo said. "I didn't think much of it but then you turned up this morning and I'm starting to wonder."

Dinah tried to keep the worry from her face. "Do you know where she lives?"

CHAPTER SEVEN

Sarah lived all the way across Hexford, and Dinah ran the entire way, her boots slamming the ground and her breath hot in her throat. She dodged through the crowds, her synaesthesia rattling off sensations as she ran. Strawberry jam, chemicals, then the taste of toothpaste. The feeling of stepping through cobwebs, running her fingers over crumpled tin foil, mud between her toes. The real sounds of the town interspersed with static, snatches of song and falling water.

She couldn't help but notice the long queue of people at the bus stop, looking back and forth down the road as if they might see the bus appear at any minute. But no one would be leaving Hexford today, it seemed.

Sarah's place was a flat over a little corner shop. Dinah hammered on the door that gave access to the flat, but it swung open under her hand to reveal an unlit hallway and stairs, a pair of kicked-off trainers in the middle of the floor and a stack of mail dumped on a side table, unopened.

Dinah hovered for a moment on the threshold. These things were sacred, after all. If she expected everyone - and everything - else to respect the simplest magical accords, then she had to abide by them as well. That meant not entering uninvited.

"Sarah?" she called out.

Nothing.

"Sarah, it's Dinah Nye." She thought about what to say next and couldn't bring herself to say, 'the Witch of Kallin Beck'. That was her mother, after all, even if she wasn't there right now. Instead, she said, apologetically, "I live at Kallin Beck cottage?"

Still nothing.

"Oh hell," she muttered, and stepped inside. If there was ever a time to argue for bending the rules, it was when someone might be in danger. Still, when she stepped over the threshold, she felt her ears pop as if from a pressure change and she swayed on the doormat as her knack fell completely silent, knocking her off balance both inside and out. There were no sensations from the passersby outside the open door. The stairwell leading up to the flat just smelled of the slightly dusty carpet and the wet coats hanging on one wall. Dinah almost turned around to leave. For all those times her knack threatened to drown her, now that it was silent she doubted whether she wanted to go into Sarah's flat without it. If there was a curse or a creature up there, now that she'd broken one of the accords and had sacrificed her magic while she was in this place, she wouldn't be able to sense it coming.

Despite it all, Dinah found her boot on the bottom stair and climbed with one hand trailing the wall of the narrow flight. At the top she rounded a corner and was faced with another door, this one visibly ajar as if someone had bustled through with armfuls of shopping and hadn't been able to push it to behind them. She felt no secondary threshold as she eased the door aside and stepped in, peering around to get a lay of the space. A kitchenette was behind a half wall to her left, with a small two-seat dining table pressed up against it. There was no breakfast on the table, no telltale morning mug. The sink was full of dirty pots. Around the door, Dinah could see that she was walking straight into the living room. She cast her eye around the small space, noting the little clusters of scented candles on the mantelpiece, the cushions and blankets piled high to make the old wicker-frame sofa more comfortable. But her attention was drawn to the only other door, presumably the bedroom, where she really expected to find Sarah.

Sunlight poured in through open curtains, there were no clothes piled on the single chair in the corner of the room, and the bed was still made up. No one had slept in there overnight. Even without her knack, a realisation hit Dinah and she backed out of the room again, casting her eye back to the pile of blankets and cushions on the sofa. She finally spotted the patch of skin under a worn-out sock heel sticking out from under the blankets.

"Sarah?" It came out in a useless whisper and Dinah had to swallow hard before trying again.

"Sarah, it's Dinah Nye."

No movement at all. The blankets were hiding any rise and fall of breath or sounds of deep sleep. Dinah crept forward, put a hand on top of the blankets, and gave them a gentle shake. Still nothing. She repeated the name again, louder, and peeled back the top blanket as if she was removing a painful plaster.

There was Sarah, her spikey blonde hair streaked with pink, still wearing her outside clothes. She had collapsed into sleep so fast, it seemed, that she hadn't bothered to close either door or make it to the bedroom. In one last effort to wake the bus driver, Dinah stroked the stranger's hair. No response. Dinah's hand slipped down to Sarah's neck. It was as warm as toast - but there was no pulse.

Dinah's hands wrapped around the scolding hot teacup without flinching.

Baker's hands, Eshe thought again. Or maybe Dinah just wanted to feel anything other than the memory of Sarah's still body under her hand. And she had felt it heightened with her knack nullified by the flat's threshold.

Everyone had convened at Charlie and Theo's place after the police brought Dinah back. Eshe realised that there were no local police in Hexford when one of the constables mentioned they'd had a hell of a time finding the place. But she, too, had struggled to find it on her first visit. Maps showed it differently depending on which one she checked, and Google Earth showed an empty field where it should have been. It was as if the village was somehow geographically debatable, which was nonsense, of course. It was just too small and too quiet to really matter in a part of Yorkshire where one small village was much like another, peppered all along a snake's nest of old roads.

With his arms wrapped around himself and Theo by his side, Charlie stood in the living room. It was easier to stay awake when you had to be on your feet.

Meredith kept moving to the kitchen sink to splash her face with cold water.

"Dinah, what do we do now?" Eshe asked.

"I—" Dinah began, as if to admit that she didn't know, but she looked between the exhausted and worried faces of her friends and changed her mind. It was no time to admit defeat when they were relying on her. "We take everyone back to Kallin Beck. It tried to get in last night and couldn't. Mer and Charlie will be safe."

"If that was the same thing," Eshe added.

"Even if it wasn't, the cottage won't let anything in."

Eshe looked deep into her friend's eyes just before Dinah snatched her gaze away. She had so many questions, but she didn't want to ask them in front of everyone else.

At one end of the room Theo shook Charlie's shoulder as his husband began to sway on his feet. At the other, Meredith's face dripped with frigid water.

"We have to do something," Dinah said. "And we know that you're not safe here. We have books and stuff back home. And we can keep an eye on each other, at least."

"No brainer," Meredith cut in, rubbing more cold water on the nape of her neck. "Between being in a safe place while we figure this out or waiting here for whatever it is to get us like- like Sarah."

Charlie nodded drowsily. He smacked his lips, his mouth dry despite the cups of coffee he'd been mainlining since they had arrived.

"If you think the answer is at Kallin Beck then that's where we'll go. I want this thing dead." Theo gripped his husband's shoulder, but Charlie gently removed his hand as he continued: "This thing killed our friend. I want it dead, Dinah."

Eshe watched Dinah's face closely as her expression cycled through fear, shock, and then resignation.

"I'll do everything I can."

Chapter Eight

When the sun rose over the forest, there was a brief, tingling moment when Isolde forgot everything weighing on her. Sitting outside her tent beside a meagre fire with her sleeping bag wrapped around her shoulders, she let her body dissolve into relaxation. Reaching down from the little spongy pad she sat on to save her bum from getting wet, her fingers wiggled down into the soil as if she was setting down roots, rewarding her with the warm sensation of the earth's magic. Her eyes lost focus as her mind drifted out on the glittering morning mist between the trees, down to where the Kallin Beck cut through the forest. She followed the stream downhill, down past the cottage that had spurned her last night, down through the village where it widened at the bridge, and out again where it turned into a larger rivulet which in turn emptied out into the shifting mirror of a lake. There, she lingered for a while, watching the kiss-like ripples on the water. Beautiful. Worth the pause and the deep breath where she smelled the water even where she still sat. But that wasn't her final destination. Down into the lake she sank gently, letting the water take her weight and lay her down like a loving mother on the rich, dark silt at the lake's bottom. The sunlight cast spears down into the murk and the bellies of fish danced through the water above her head. The shadows of old drowned branches in the gloom seemed so restful with their lazy arches and slumbering branches, and she willed herself to be as still as them, to just enjoy the peace of not being found at the lake bottom.

Her mother's voice came like a klaxon, shattering Isolde's concentration and snapping her back into herself.

"We are waiting."

Jumping up, Isolde grabbed her jacket and jogged through the forest, finger combing her hair and trying to neaten the dark make-up under her eye with a wet finger. Without a mirror the work was speculative at best, and it frankly didn't make her feel any more prepared.

There was no clearing out that way, and the edge of the forest was far off, Isolde just knew the meeting place between the trees by the pricking of her palms, the breath of cold breeze through her hair.

"Where were you?"

"Sorry, Mother. I was meditating."

Amabel Tanner suddenly stood in the space between two mossy trees, her back to her daughter, regarding the forest. Her hair was the same black as Isolde's own but long around her shoulders. If she had turned around, Isolde would have been able to see the splash of grey that outlined her mother's face.

"I suppose you were in some bog or under a rock," Mother Tanner said in a pointed tone.

"Oh Mother, leave her be. Our Isolde likes to keep her own peace."

Isolde's elder sister, Lucia, stood where she hadn't been a moment ago, one hand resting on a huge fallen trunk. She was her mother's double, with only time and the twists in her dark hair serving to tell them apart. Her long black velveteen dress spread out onto the ground around her. She picked something from the mossy bark at her side, regarded it, and dusted it from her fingers.

If Isolde had chided their mother in the same way, however gently, there would have been fireworks for weeks. But this was Lucia and so the comment passed. Mother Tanner simply turned to her daughters and changed the subject, her long, black shift dress overlaid with silver necklaces making no sound, nor disturbing the ground as she moved.

"What progress at Kallin Beck?"

Isolde looked around herself, waiting for her other, younger sister to appear somewhere. But she didn't.

"Isolde, I asked you a question."

"Good. Good progress," Isolde said. "My invisibility spell works extremely well. They can't see me at all."

"Less about your own projects, child. Have you gained access to the cottage or not?"

Isolde swallowed. "No, Mother."

"What's stopping you?"

"The cottage, its wards are formidable—"

"There is no reason why the cottage shouldn't allow you access as a fellow witch of benign intent," Amabel recited.

Isolde had heard this before, in the meagre brief she had been given before being sent to Hexford. She didn't mention that the cottage had knocked her on her bruised arse the night before. Mother Tanner would have no such excuses and it would be a waste of breath.

"I'll try harder," was all she said.

"There should be no need. Succeed on the first try."

The old Tanner adage from her mother's lips made Isolde shudder. Instead of replying, she simply hung her head as Mother Tanner carried on, "If that house falls, Chaos will follow. Get inside. Assess the damage already done."

Silence fell, and strung out. When Isolde dared look up, she realised that her mother had disappeared without a word of farewell.

"She thinks she's Batman," Lucia said with a barely-there smile. Her eyes were dark and glistening, almost emotionless to anyone not used to the Tanner ways. Only Vivian was allowed to express high emotions without being chided, the younger sister being of an irrepressibly chaotic temperament.

That brought Isolde to what had been on her mind through the entire conversation. The Tanner family coven had three witches, mother and two daughters, tellingly not including Isolde herself. But Vivian wasn't there.

"Where's Vivian? Is she unwell?" she asked,

hoping that her youngest sister had simply been permitted to continue her latest painting rather than meet with Isolde.

"She remains lost in visions," replied Lucia, the cryptic flatness of the phrase indicating to Isolde that it was one of her mother's. "Her paintings are becoming more- abstract. Her gift is getting worse."

"Maybe I can help decipher them. I'd like to see Viv," Isolde offered. "If Mother ever lets me return home from these constant errands."

Lucia's tight jaw and sad eyes spoke volumes, but she said nothing.

"Why's Mother so obsessed with this cottage, Luce? It's just a couple of country witches in a particularly well warded house."

"Two witches are as good as no witches at all." Another of Mother's catchphrases and one that Isolde had vocally disagreed with in the past. Plenty of lone practitioners were extremely effective and even powerful. Not that her mother would ever see it Isolde's way. It was the Coven way or the highway for Amabel Tanner.

Lucia's head twitched to the side. "She's calling. Really do try, Iz."

She was gone in the space between Isolde's blinks. Although she was certain that they were gone, Isolde looked around her anyway, calming her mind to feel for the sense of someone watching, for the tingle of residual magic. She felt nothing. She was alone again.

CHAPTER NINE

"Alright, everyone in the circle."

Eshe had checked her notebooks, then rechecked them, and now she stood with one open in her hand, a piece of chalk in the other.

It was easy enough for Mer, Charlie and even Theo to fit inside the circle with a bedroll and sleeping bag each, as they had moved all of the Kallin Beck dining room furniture aside, piling it high, in order to make as much room as possible. In reality, it was three circles overlapping, a Venn diagram with the largest possible section in the centre. This particular design Eshe hadn't learned from Kallin Beck cottage, it was an amalgamation of many apotropaic marks that she'd studied for years. But all that had been academic. This had to work in practice.

Eshe looked from her book to her circle and back.

"I have no idea what I'm doing," she muttered so that only Dinah could hear.

"It looks brilliant," Dinah said as Eshe stepped back from her work. "Like a proper witch."

"It seems right that there be three interconnected circles as there are three people connected by- whatever this is. If it needs something else, I'm not sure what." She flicked back and forth a few pages. "There are too many options."

Dinah pursed her lips thoughtfully. "These things can be as complex or simple as you like, really. We could add candles, salt, all kinds of things, but in the end it's the intent of the witch that really matters."

"So, what do we do now? Does it just work?"

Dinah shrugged. "I usually like to touch something, like my dough, and think about what I want people to feel when they eat it. Kind of push your intentions into it a little, let your work know what your aim is, give it a little direction."

"That's it?"

Dinah gave her a tight-lipped, apologetic look. "That's as easy and hard as it ever needs to be, if that's how you want to work."

"So, can you touch the lines and make them magic?" she asked.

Dinah took her friend's hand and led her down to her knees beside the circles. "We both can."

Reaching out a finger, Dinah touched one of the lines with a fingertip. Eshe copied her, but snapped her hand back a few seconds later when Dinah pushed a little mote of intent into the circle. She looked at her hand, and ran her thumb across her fingers.

Dinah grinned. Eshe had felt it, for sure.

"And that's that. Even if something gets into the cottage, which I'm confident it won't, then it'll have to get through the extra protection of your circles as well."

"Can we have a book or something?" Theo asked, sitting cross legged in the circle. "It'll be a long night otherwise."

"Or we could sleep," Charlie suggested grumpily.

Dinah smiled. "You should be able to sleep safely now. Maybe that's not such a bad idea?"

Mer and Charlie, at least, settled down to sleep. Theo lay in his sleeping bag but stared at the exposed beams of the ceiling rather than closing his eyes. Dinah and Eshe moved off to one side of the room, armfuls of books between them.

"We don't know anything new," Eshe whispered as she checked her spider diagrams and lists from the night before.

Dinah opened a book, seemingly to a random page, but didn't really read. "Not much. But whatever happened to Sarah, her flat's threshold didn't stop it. It sure drained all the magic out of me though."

Eshe dropped her voice. "Wait, you said the cottage is safer."

"Kallin Beck isn't just a regular threshold. You've seen yourself how many enchantments have been laid over this place, year after year, overlapping and working together, the will of who-knows-how-many witches fermenting for centuries. This is the safest place in the world for those three right now. I just wish we'd known about Sarah earlier. If I'd have asked more questions, maybe. Or if I just knew more, like Mum does, I'd have been able to save her."

There were no words that would have given Dinah any comfort. Eshe reached out and gripped her hand instead. "We'll figure this out. We just need to know a little more. Anything might help."

Dinah grabbed a notepad and drew a circle on the page. In the middle she wrote, 'connections'.

"Alright. Let's do one of your brainstorming rituals," she said. Eshe looked confused, drawing a smile from Dinah. "What about these spider diagrams isn't a ritual? Circles, connecting lines, paths of thought connecting ideas, moving toward an outcome that will help us."

"That's a spider graph."

Dinah held up a finger. "That's a ritual. Everyday magic, right under your nose."

Eshe looked down at the page, then back at Dinah, and something dawned behind her eyes, something that Dinah had been waiting for months to see. A little flicker of real belief. The student took the notepad gently as if she was seeing it for the first time. As they talked, lines spiralled out, circles were drawn, connected, and a complex divination of thought appeared across the page.

"They all live in Hexford. They're friends so they're personally connected as well."

"And they all provide services to the public?" Dinah added.

"That's a good point. Food, knowledge, transport."

Out came more explosions of lines and connections.

"Could it be nothing to do with these three, but something toying with Hexford itself? Trying to shut down the town for some kind of mischief."

"Devilment turned deadly," Eshe muttered solemnly, adding another circle with 'Hexford' at its centre.

"That could make it very hard to find this thing, and it could just go find someone else to bother. A crossing guard, a greengrocer." Dinah paused. Her Dad. She had been supposed to see him yesterday but had been turned back by Meredith's problem. He was the town baker, providing food to so many people across Hexford. Dinah wanted to jump up out of her chair, run out of the door, and go to him straight away. Flashes of him lying in the bakery, alone and dead as Sarah had been, flashed through her head.

"What's wrong?"

Dinah's eye was drawn slowly to her friends slumbering in the circle. Even Theo had dropped off.

"Nothing," she said. "We just need to work fast, is all. Just in case this thing decides to pick on someone else."

Hours passed, the sun slipped across the sky and down toward the horizon. The notepad filled with more connections, books were skimmed and discarded, and still the witches were no closer to an answer. Dinah made tea for everyone when the sleepers woke, a regular brew with her uncanny intent for protection and calm placed over it.

Charlie and Meredith actually looked better. The grey had drawn out of their faces, and their voices were clearer, words less slurred.

"I feel like dog dirt," Charlie muttered, sipping his tea. Meredith nodded silently.

"Are we any closer to an answer?" Theo asked, eyeing the darkening windows.

Dinah and Eshe exchanged glances.

"Honestly? There's just no more information. We need- something." Dinah said. Her own tea had grown a cold scab on top where she'd left it.

"What else is there? We're friends," Meredith said, pausing before adding: "We were all friends with Sarah."

"What about your camping trip?" Theo added. "That was about a month back."

Dinah's head snapped up.

Curious looks passed over Charlie and Meredith's faces.

"What camping trip?" Charlie said.

Theo looked from one to the other. "You all went up to the Tor."

"And you didn't go?" Eshe asked.

"I was visiting my Mum in Huddersfield," Theo replied. "Charlie here wangled his way out of it."

A look passed between Charlie and Meredith: sleepy eyes and slow blinks.

"I'm drawing a blank," Meredith said. "We made plans, didn't we? I remember that. But- did we actually go?"

Charlie just looked at her wild-eyed.

Dinah was already scrambling at her books. "Something must have followed you back from the Tor, something wandering around up there. Maybe a wandering spirit."

"Can ghosts just follow people home?" Eshe asked with a shudder.

"Imagine you're a regular person who gets lost out on the dales. It happens all the time. It's dangerous out there. So, you die—" Everyone exchanged worried looks, apart from Dinah who was fumbling at the books, talking faster. "And you can't find your way home any more than you could when you were alive. You're left wandering the dales for eternity, until you stumble across three warm bodies. Three real-life people. And you haven't seen another real-life person for—" Dinah gestured expansively. "—who knows? But they still can't see you. So, when they go, you follow them home. All of a sudden, you're back in a real village, with living, breathing people. It's what you've been craving. Only now you're surrounded by people, and you still can't feel anything. So, you make a connection the only way you can. How are you supposed to know that sharing warmth drags the living closer to you than you to them?"

"Flaming hell, Dinah." Meredith whispered.

Dinah's eyes cleared and she finished lamely, "Or, you know, something like that."

"How do we bust a ghost?" Theo asked. "We can't even see this thing, can we?"

"It's ok, it's ok," Dinah said. She wasn't sure if she was calming her friends or herself. "We can still do something about it. We're sure it's a thing, now. That means it can be caught."

"Caught?" Theo interrupted. "How do we kill it?"

"He's right, Dinah. This thing killed someone. What's to stop it just coming back?" Eshe said softly.

"No." Dinah stood up, paced away from the table, around the outskirts of the protection circle. "We don't kill things. We send them packing. That's all we can do."

Charlie opened his mouth to add something, but Dinah cut him off.

"No, Charlie. I hate what happened to Sarah as much as you do. I really do. I'm supposed to be the one protecting Hexford from things like this after all. But we do not destroy. It's one of the old accords. It's there for a reason."

"Then what do we do?" Eshe asked, reminding herself to ask more about the 'accords' later.

Dinah stopped dead, her mouth half open. Damn, she had just been spouting her mother's words, hadn't she? It was almost as if she had been in the room. After a moment she said, "Everyone get some rest. You're safe as long as you're inside the cottage. And I need a recipe."

She darted into the kitchen and Eshe followed, casting a glance back at her uncertain friends. To the casual eye, it looked like Dinah had just lost her marbles.

"Urm, Dinah?" Eshe began, her tone betraying her thoughts.

"We know it'll be visiting two places tonight, so we just stake out one."

"Stake out?" Eshe said with a chuckle.

"I watch too much TV, don't I? Anyway, I think Theo's caught onto something. He should have seen this thing when Charlie was affected, right? If it could be seen. But he didn't. So, it's invisible."

Eshe nodded uncertainly. "That makes sense. Well, not exactly sense—"

Slapping her recipe book down on the kitchen's wooden island, Dinah started to flip through. "So, we need something to help us see it. I don't think I have a spell for that. We both know that's not my thing. So, we need to make something that will make it visible."

"Like a marinade?" Eshe asked.

Laughing as she moved around the kitchen, Dinah

collected a large mason jar, an armful of herbs and other ingredients, stale bread from the breadboard, and an ancient pestle and mortar that took two hands to lift.

"Kind of. It's more of a dredge. We don't want to have to rub it on and wait overnight." Dinah's tone was breezy again now that she was in her kitchen. She started to crush ingredients in the pestle and mortar and add them to the jar. Eshe got the distinct feeling that while Dinah was speaking aloud, it wasn't really to her - even though she was the only other person there. The kitchen witch was just talking herself through her new recipe.

"Crumble up the stale bread to make breadcrumbs, because we know that breadcrumbs always lead you where you want to go. Black pepper opens the third eye and exorcises negative emotions. Onion for collecting the negative energy and showing it the door. Cayenne pepper removes blockages and barriers. Salt is good for all kinds of stuff, really. Always better to add a bit. Garlic for driving away evil spirits."

"You're making my mouth water," Eshe said. "What's the paprika for?"

"Oh." Dinah looked at her hand, which was stained a smoky red, as if she didn't really remember how it got that way. Everything had been instinct and experience. "I just like paprika."

Eshe buzzed with excitement. Her friend seemed so focussed now, and that made Eshe feel a lot more confident as well.

"So, we throw this stuff on the creature, and it becomes visible. Then what?"

"Urm." Dinah looked around then ducked under

the island, returning with an empty potato sack in hand.

Eshe's confidence dipped ever so slightly. "You're kidding."

CHAPTER TEN

By the time the shadows had gathered under the trees, Isolde was waiting. There was a brief period where the internal lights were switched on, but the curtains were yet to be closed, and she had an uninterrupted view of the goings-on inside Kallin Beck Cottage. She had to circle around the house in order to see inside all of the rooms and get a really good read on things, but it seemed like the two witches had invited others to perform some rite. There were five of them in total. Books that Isolde would kill to read were passed back and forth, and they all seemed immersed in chatter. Desperate to know what they were talking about, another part of Isolde was even more desperate to be involved. It also hurt a little that the cottage had let in these newcomers but that it had rebounded her on principle. Clearly the wards were less static than she had first assumed.

She could have pushed a little power into eavesdropping. There was an old incantation, half remembered, that she might be able to use for a quick and nasty spell. But she was saving all of her energy for her invisibility should it be needed.

That was another thing. As far as she could tell, these witches never actually did anything. There was a lot of talk, a lot of reading, and the Kallin Beck witch seemed to cook all the time, but there was no actual magic being used. None of them exerted any power that Isolde could feel. No spells were wrought, no invocations uttered. She was starting to wonder if her mother had not only been right but whether the situation was even worse than anticipated. There seemed to be no witches in Kallin Beck at all. And if that were true, if only the cottage itself had any real power, then it was a magical time bomb. Such a powerful yet inanimate object always needed guardians, guides. And those guides should be powerful in their own right, knowledgeable in their craft. The Kallin Beck witch and her friend seemed pleasant, but a kind heart wasn't enough when it came to old magic. You needed wisdom, too.

But all Isolde had to do was assess and report back. Was the cottage in good hands or not? So far, she was thinking not.

While she was thinking this over, deciding whether to despair or rejoice - for either way her errand would be over soon - the front door swung open and out walked the Kallin Beck witch and her friend. Both were bundled up against the chill evening and the Kallin Beck witch carried a large mason jar under her arm. Everyone else seemed to be staying behind. Isolde looked from the cottage to the witches' retreating backs and decided to follow rather than attempt another entry. Maybe she could overhear something that would give her a useful insight.

With her back to a shadow-soaked tree, Isolde summoned her will. The feeling began at her feet and passed through her boot heels into her calves and then spread through her chest and face like a blush. She wrapped her right hand around her left wrist where the leather braid and trefoil charm helped her focus her concentration. Gently, politely, she asked the light to step around her, and gave a wry smile as the light agreed. A little chill ran through her as she stepped out into the night to catch up with the witches.

Down the old track to Hexford they went, the road easy to follow even when clouds passed over the sickle moon. The Kallin Beck witch hugged her jar and seemed focussed on little else. The other witch kept looking over her shoulder, and for a moment Isolde thought that she had followed too closely. Her spell only covered her visually, she could still be heard. Just in case, she hung back a little more.

At night, Hexford was a quiet place. Warm light spilled out into the street from lattice windows, and the night breeze had the pleasant honey and vanilla smell of Night Phlox. Isolde had to admit that Hexford had the sweetest nights she had ever experienced. She was hard pressed not to stare up at the moon or drift off on some nocturnal wandering, to just enjoy the blanket of night wrapped around her.

The witches took a side street and at first it seemed as if they might be headed for the library. But instead they dived deeper into Hexford's knot of streets until they stood on a gentle cobbled hill. They stopped on one side of the road in the light of a chip shop window, watching a narrow house across the way. Isolde dared creep closer, confident that the light wouldn't reveal her. The only danger of discovery would come from the rumbling of her stomach as she smelled the fish and chip fog that gathered in the street.

"We don't want to spook it," the Kallin Beck witch said.

"Do you think you can sense it from out here?" the other asked.

The Kallin Beck witch muttered something and started to preen the long brown braid of her hair, straightening her chunky cardigan.

"What's wrong? Oh, wait," her friend said with a sly smile. "Lover boy's around somewhere, isn't he?"

"Give up. Please," Dinah said with a chuckle.

Isolde realised that the Kallin Beck witch must have some kind of gift. An extra sense. That made Isolde step back a little and she almost collided with a young man coming out of the chip shop, who obviously had no idea she was there.

With messy black hair, light brown skin, and a strong shaven chin, he was good-looking without being sculpted in any way. His open jacket showed a layered t-shirt and shirt underneath and a gold kara was visible on his wrist. Carrying an open tray of chips, fishcake, and gravy, he prodded his meal with a little wooden fork that was better for splitting the chips apart than spearing them.

Isolde took another step back from the group to watch.

"Eshe, Dinah," the young man said with a little surprised smile on his lips. "Want a chip?"

On the sidelines, Isolde noted the new names. Names had power and she instantly knew that the risk of following the witches had been worth learning theirs.

"No thank you," Dinah said timidly.

Eshe leaned in to grab one with as much gravy as possible. "Hiya, Hari. Can't pass up one of Danny's chips."

"Best I've ever tasted," Hari said, eating another. "I'm sure he puts crack in the gravy."

Dinah giggled and Eshe glanced at her sideways with a barely concealed smirk.

"I heard about Sarah, and that you were there, Dinah. So sorry," Hari said. "Do you know what happened?"

Dinah's demeanour changed, she seemed to bristle as she said curtly, "No."

Hari held up a hand. "I'm not fishing. I already wrote a piece and it's off to print. Scant details, just a really sad accident."

"Yeah," Dinah sighed. "Sorry. It's just—"

"Yeah, I bet," he replied sadly.

Both Dinah and Hari exchanged sad kinds of smiles. Dinah brushed a strand of hair behind her ear. Hari wiped the corner of his mouth with his thumb in case he had gravy stored there.

Eshe rolled her eyes at them both. "We don't know, Hari. That's the truth."

"But you're out here investigating, aren't you?" he replied.

Dinah and Eshe exchanged looks. Hari's lips grew tight and pale.

"Good. Kick its arse. I didn't know Sarah well or anything, but she always seemed nice," he said, turning away. He took a few steps before turning back. He was looking at Dinah when he said, "And be careful. Please? Both of you."

Eshe gave an exaggerated wink, which drew a sad smile from Hari before he sauntered off down the street.

Isolde watched the whole thing play out, marking this Hari as a new player in their lives. It was obvious that the Kallin Beck witch, Dinah, fancied the journalist. Isolde rolled her eyes. *So obvious.*

Eshe poked Dinah in the ribs. "You're rubbish."

"My mind's on other things right now."

"You don't need your mind on him, Dinah." Eshe did a little mock dance and sang, "It's your bodaaay."

Dinah's face turned a bright shade of purple.

"What sense do you get off of him? Is it a smell? Or a sensation?"

"None of your business!" Dinah replied, turning half away from her friend.

"Oooh. It *is* a sensation, then."

"Give over," Dinah muttered. "We're supposed to be keeping an eye out."

Eshe let it drop but the interaction had confirmed a few of Isolde's guesses. Mainly, that the locals of Hexford knew exactly what Dinah and Eshe were, that they knew at least a little about magical matters and their existence, and that the townsfolk were confident in the Kallin Beck witch. That confidence didn't come from nowhere. Isolde eyed Dinah again. Maybe she was just very good at hiding her true power, which was a formidable skill in itself.

CHAPTER ELEVEN

Dinah tingled with magic from shoulders to fingertips as she hugged the mason jar filled with her revealing dredge. Hari turning up had thrown her off a little, and she found herself pushing her concentration in his direction until he was out of range of her knack. She told herself it was to make sure that he was out of harm's way, but she secretly craved the sensation of putting on warm, fleecy socks that he brought to her toes.

Eshe's good-natured jabbing had actually helped her to focus. Being in Hexford was swamping her knack as always but she had to concentrate it on Meredith's house to make sure that she sensed anything changing inside straight away. Dinah had no clue how the thing that was draining her friends would get in or out, but at least she might feel it when it did appear. It was bugging her that this thing apparently ignored the threshold. Even ghosts should have been affected by entering and exiting someone else's home. The only explanation Dinah could think of was that this thing was so powerful that the old accords made no difference to it, or it was so rare that the rules didn't take it into account. Both options were incredibly worrying. If this thing was so powerful, there was nothing she'd be able to do to stop it, and if it was outside of the accords for some other reason, she had no idea where to even start looking for answers. And how many more people could die while she was looking?

The night was mild, as always, and the smell from the chip shop was maddeningly alluring as they waited and waited. But as the sickle moon reached its zenith, the sensation of her ears popping pushed through all the other stimuli assaulting Dinah. Reflexively she tried to clear it by yawning, but the feeling didn't budge. It was as if she'd taken a hike up on the ridges over Hexford, the altitude muffling her ears.

"It's here," she said, and Eshe had to run to keep up as Dinah stalked over the road.

Meredith had given them the old iron key to her front door and so the witches slipped inside without Dinah's powers dissipating at the threshold and without the magic leaching from the mason jar. Stepping further into the living room, the many sensations of Hexford fell away at the door and Dinah could concentrate a little better. The sensation of pressure, like something displacing the air inside Meredith's house, was accompanied by the taste of liquorice, the same that Dinah had felt through the cottage door at Kallin Beck the night before. That was worrying. Only once before had her knack allocated two sensations to a single thing. The liquorice was likely the creature, but she had a nasty feeling that the pressure might be coming from some kind of ongoing spell.

"It's here. I can taste liquorice again," Dinah said. She didn't mention that she'd never known a creature to give her multiple sensations, or that she had no idea what that meant. She didn't want to spook Eshe any more than she already was.

Eshe, who had been holding open the door in case they had to make a hasty escape, finally clicked it closed. They were in there with whatever it was for good or ill, now.

"Upstairs?" she whispered.

Dinah nodded distractedly. The sensations of the creature were all around her and it was hard to pin its position down, but the bedroom seemed like the place to start. With Dinah and the mason jar in front, they climbed the stairs, which creaked and groaned way more than they should have. Dinah swallowed, trying to flush the taste of liquorice from her mouth with no success. The pressure in her ears grew until they were ringing. Something was definitely in there, definitely close.

Eshe scooched around Dinah in the narrow hallway, putting herself on the opposite side of Meredith's bedroom door as if she was a TV cop. Dinah reached into the mason jar, taking a handful of the revealing dredge, nodded to her friend, and Eshe slowly swung open the door.

With the curtains drawn back and moonlight casting a single search beam across the dark, they could have been stepping into a vampire's crypt or a ghost's attic, but for the comfy little bed with rumpled bed clothes and knitted blankets, the pile of clothes on the floor, and the soft scent of lavender from the unlit candles on the windowsill.

Dinah stepped inside in a way that she hoped looked bolder than it felt. The hand holding the dredge was shaking, and her knees felt like they wanted to stay at the door while the rest of her went inside. But Eshe was so close behind her that she could feel her, and one hand was on her shoulder. They were together and Dinah could feel the sensation of Eshe like popping candy in her mouth, another welcome little anchor.

Between the two witches, they scanned every corner that they could, even though they weren't entirely sure what they were looking for. From their research, Eshe had some old woodcuts flashing through her head of creatures she definitely never wanted to meet. Dinah was trying to imagine both how small and large this thing could be, whether it would be hiding, or whether it might be that the creature was the very shadows they crept through. She tried to expect the appearance of an apparition so that she wouldn't jump when it came, but only succeeded in increasing her anxiety instead. The sound of their breathing seemed to fill the perfectly still room alongside the pressure and growing taste of liquorice.

Dinah didn't know why, but she reacted to the corner of the room. Drawing her hand from the mason jar in one fluid motion she scattered the revealing dredge into the air in that direction. The creature was faster, and only a rear haunch ending in a two-toed foot appeared out of thin air.

"That's not a ghost," Dinah whispered, her voice rising with panic as she shoved her hand back into the jar.

It was on the move, but now Dinah had something to aim for and her next handful filled the air, manifesting the creature in its scuttling entirety. With glistening green skin, its face long with bulging, milky eyes, there was something of a flayed wallaby to its appearance. It must have realised the jig was up because the creature dangled from the curtains and hissed before bounding off across the room, this time landing on the bed.

Eshe thumped into the chest of drawers behind her, her eyes wide and breath ragged. She clutched the potato sack like a talisman, and froze with only her eyes darting wherever the creature bounded.

"Eshe, the sack!" Dinah danced around in circles, trying to keep her eyes on the acrobatic creature as it knocked over a photo frame, shattered a mirror, and tried to jump out of the closed window before bouncing back from the glass like a gigantic fly.

But Eshe wasn't moving. Up until the moment that the thing had become visible there had been a large portion of her that was just playing along with Dinah. Her friend was lovely, but deluded. If chasing invisible creatures made her feel better, then that's what they'd do. And then the damned thing had turned out to be real and now Eshe had to tear her fingers away from her last handhold on an old reality. This stuff really was real. She'd seen it now. She was done for.

Dinah was looking back at her, a worried expression on her face.

"I'm ok," Eshe said too quietly for her to be speaking to Dinah, but she still didn't move. "It's just like a trapped pigeon. Or a mouse. Just have to put it in the bag."

Knuckles pale on the potato sack, she stepped slowly forward and, making a half-hearted swipe, missed the scuttling thing entirely on her first try. Dinah put herself in the doorway, arms wide, as the creature bolted toward the exit. As it was turned back, the creature gave a throaty trill and tried to somersault backward, but Eshe was behind it already and the sack went over the creature's head mostly by accident. Bundling it inside and bear hugging the struggling sack, she fought to keep hold of it, but the imp soon gave up all hope of escape.

"Well that went alr—-" Eshe began to say, but she was interrupted when Dinah let out a wordless yelp of surprise. Looking back, Eshe saw that the revealing dredge had also revealed something else.

In the corner of the room there now stood a young woman with tousled dark hair. As Dinah and Eshe both turned to regard her, she looked at her hands, down to her feet, and realisation dawned on her pale face. With a raspy sigh, she slowly raised her hands.

CHAPTER TWELVE

It was the indignity of being manhandled that really annoyed Isolde. The Kallin Beck witches grabbed her, dragging her down the stairs. Remaining invisible for so long had left her with weak knees and drained of energy, and so there was very little she could do to put up a fight. But what really irked her was that they hadn't even bothered to tie her up. They clearly didn't see her as particularly dangerous, or as a threat, when they plonked her down at Meredith's dining room table like a naughty child. Even the creature was treated with more respectful caution - and that was currently snoring in its potato sack.

Both witches just stood there, arms folded, scowling at her like disappointed mothers. She knew the look all too well.

"Alright, the jig is up," Eshe snapped, sounding like some 1920s detective, an instant giveaway that this was her first interrogation. "What is this thing and why are you hurting our friends?"

"You're the witches of the famous Kallin Beck," Isolde muttered. "You tell me."

"We're not. Not really," Dinah said timidly. She kept working her mouth as if she was trying to dislodge a bad taste.

"You are, Dinah." Eshe found herself rocking the creature in its bag like a baby. It just felt right while it was asleep. She turned to Isolde. "I'm just staying for a bit."

"The witch of Kallin Beck is my Mum. She's in Finland with her coven."

Isolde shook her head. "You waste so much effort denying a powerful gift. As soon as she left, you inherited it. As she did from her mother, and she from hers. You should both know that there's more to inheritance than bricks and mortar. With inheritance come blessings, good and bad."

Eshe eyed Dinah. "Are we being lectured?"

Dinah didn't reply, instead saying, "Please empty your pockets onto the table. Slowly."

Isolde did as she was told, laying all kinds of trinkets and curiosities onto the table. "You have no need to worry. You shorted out my spell with your dust. I don't have enough magic left to blow my nose, never mind disappear."

"It isn't disappearing that I'm worried about," Dinah muttered mostly to herself.

She started to sift through the contents of Isolde's pockets. A hag stone, tightly bundled and bound twine, a tiny wooden effigy of Hecate with her three faces pointing in different directions, half of a flapjack still in its wrapper, and more odds and ends than a kitchen drawer. There was also a thin notebook, scuffed at the corners, which Eshe reached for. She read the inscription on the cover.

"Isolde Tanner."

A smile crept across Isolde's lips as if the name was about to elicit some reaction from her captors. When the Kallin Beck witches just exchanged blank looks, Isolde let out a disappointed sigh.

"What is this?" Eshe asked. "Spells?"

"Poetry," Isolde muttered.

"You write poetry?"

"A little."

Eshe leafed through the pages. It was a lot. She read some more carefully, and some she even read twice. "This is really good."

For the first time Isolde seemed caught off guard. First her eyes widened, then narrowed as she thought she saw deceit where there wasn't any. She said nothing. No amount of compliments would make her drop her guard.

"And now, I suppose you're going to kill me," she said, gathering her composure.

Dinah and Eshe exchanged shocked looks.

"Bloody hell, Isolde. No," Eshe said.

Dinah added, "For the record, we don't destroy. We don't kill. We maintain balance."

"I'm told it's a big rule," Eshe added.

Isolde recognised a mantra handed down and repeated, she and her sisters did the same all too often. That really was the Kallin Beck way, then.

"Then for the record," Isolde said, visibly relaxing

as the perceived threat dissipated, "I have nothing to do with the nightmare upstairs. I was following you, not summoning that. I wanted to know what you were up to with the whole jar and sneaking around thing."

That wasn't technically a lie, she thought.

"We can't just let her go, can we?" Eshe said, still holding the book of poetry.

"What else can we do? Keep her tied up in here for being nosey? I don't think Meredith's going to be too impressed. She's not some entity. She's just a witch like us. Just a regular person." Dinah turned to Isolde. "What will you do if we let you go?"

Isolde scoffed. "Go home and wallow."

Eshe snorted a laugh.

"Or you could help us," Dinah offered. "You obviously know more about spells and arcane magic than we do. I certainly can't make myself invisible. There are people being hurt here. You could help."

There was something annoyingly disarming about the Kallin Beck witch, Isolde thought. There was so little pretence with Dinah, she just said what she was thinking, expressed what she needed, laid her heart on those rolled up cardigan sleeves. Isolde wondered how much she could learn about the witches, the cottage, everything her mother wanted to know, if she just asked. Walking up to the door of Kallin Beck and asking to come in had never occurred to her.

"Maybe," was all she said, but she didn't get up from the dining table or try to leave.

Dinah's eyes slid away from the new witch as if she might swipe a paw at her. Isolde made her think of a stray cat that would bump your legs when it was hungry and then disappear for six months at a time.

"Something's bothering me," she said. "How did this thing get in without the threshold taking its power? There are things that can ignore the old accords, but they are huge, legendary, powerful things. Then there's this —" she gestured to the snoring sack. The creature had stretched out in its sleep until one taloned foot poked out of the top of the bag.

Isolde sighed. "A window left open at midnight. Sweet food left on a sill. Bluebells by an entrance. Wormwood anywhere in the house. They all imply an invitation that a nightmare can make use of."

"I checked for all of those," Dinah said. "Nothing."

Isolde's carefully expressionless mouth pursed in thought.

"There are some apotropaic marks that can maintain open connections and borders. But accidentally appearing in three houses at once?" Eshe added with a look that implied what was coming.

"Then it's intentional," Isolde said.

Dinah's face fell. "Someone is letting these-nightmares in on purpose."

"And whipping them into a frenzy. Nightmares don't kill," Isolde added. She had to try not to smile, try not to show that she was having fun. "Terrifying pests, yes. But they feed and leave."

"We need to search the whole house again. This time we're looking for intentional spellwork," Dinah said. She turned to Isolde. "It'll be well hidden. Are you going to help us?"

"I'm interested to know what's going on." Isolde said, pushing back her chair.

Eshe rolled her eyes. "I think that's as close to a

'yes' as we're going to get."

They searched every inch of the house, taking it room by room. Dinah and Isolde moved furniture, searched drawers, and found nothing but dust and old receipts. Eshe searched the doorways, windowsills, chimney, and even the rafters in the loft for any purposeful magical marks. But as the night rolled on, they found nothing. Not until Dinah checked through Meredith's many, multicoloured woollen coats. Through the worn stitching of a pocket lining, Dinah dug down into the coat itself, her fingers brushing something hard and sharp that she couldn't identify. Keys? No. A ring of some kind? It was too heavy. Drawing it out, she turned the object this way and that. Small enough to fit in her palm, it was rolled up like a little scroll, only made of dusky metal and stabbed through with a roughly made bronze nail.

Isolde appeared by her shoulder and grabbed her wrist. "Be careful with that."

"What is it?" Dinah asked.

In answer, Isolde spoke only one word, "Defixio".

Leading Dinah by her wrist to the dining table, Isolde eased Dinah's hand over until the strange little thing dropped to the tabletop with a thud, and then she let go.

"A curse tablet," she continued. "It was likely placed in a pocket and Meredith carried it in herself. Then the threshold was left open for the nightmare."

Eshe bent over, peering at the little metal scroll as if she was studying a beetle, her hands firmly behind her back. "Did a witch do this?"

"No witch I know would ever," Isolde said.

Dinah shook her head. "Me neither. I've heard of

bindings made of paper, wrapped in twine but this—"

"This magic is much older, and cast to last," Isolde muttered. "We have to open it."

Dinah's face scrunched up in surprise. "You're kidding."

"We need to know what it says."

"So how do we open it?" Eshe asked, looking at the thing like it might be a rubix cube rather than a magical object.

"Not at all, if we can help it," Dinah said.

Eshe gave her a worried glance. Isolde's expression wasn't so polite.

Dinah sighed. "Carefully, then. If we have to."

Isolde was allowed to eat the remainder of her flapjack to restore some of her magical potency. Dinah borrowed some dried herbs from Meredith's cupboard, even managing to find some dusty dried sage in a glass container, rubbing it between her hands to cleanse herself. When they had both made their preparations, Dinah and Isolde sat on opposite sides of the table.

Creating a circle of salt on the tabletop, Eshe had them lay their hands, palms up, over the line. Casting a little intent into the circle as Dinah had shown her, she sealed it.

"If I'm right, this should act like something magically akin to a hermetically sealed chemical chamber. Just don't remove your hands and anything that happens inside will stay inside."

"Unless our hands melt off, and then we won't have much of a choice," Isolde said as if the others weren't there.

"Well, that will be a whole other problem," Eshe replied with an acerbic tang.

Isolde, who had been eyeing her work carefully, cocked an eyebrow. Eshe couldn't quite tell if it signalled disdain or approval. Stepping back, Eshe made a second circle around the whole table and the two witches and stepped outside of it before activating the second protective ring.

"That should do it. I think."

Carefully focussing their intent into their fingertips, the witches went to work. Dinah lifted the metal scroll from the table with the middle finger of each hand as if she was lifting the lid on a bomb casing. Isolde muttered odd words to herself in a barely audible litany, gripped the pin between finger and thumb on both ends, and began guiding it back through the scroll. She flinched, sucking air through her teeth.

Dinah's eyes shot wide. Eshe held up her hands like she might fend off an explosion. Isolde held her seized breath.

Everyone froze.

The moment stretched out with the witches petrified in place.

"You guys ok?" Eshe asked between clenched teeth.

Isolde moved her finger away from the pin's point, a blossoming spot of blood on her fingertip.

"It appears so," she said, sounding uncertain for the first time since they'd met. Her closed black lips moved oddly as she ran her tongue around her teeth. Then, with a deep breath, she continued to extract the pin, painfully slowly. Carefully, she laid it aside.

Now it was Dinah's turn. She turned the unbound defixio this way and that between her fingertips as if checking which wire to cut, then she began to unroll it. When she was half-way through, she had to stop, her nose scrunched up. The most potent reek of wet dog was coming off the thing as it unfurled, and she could feel the unrolling of the tacky fur down her tongue. She retched, and looked at the others, but it seemed they couldn't sense it. Her knack had never given her a sensation like that before. Even when it was overwhelming, she'd never had such a visceral reaction. She carried on as best she could and soon the little lead tablet was laid out on the dining table, the markings on its surface out of place under the kitchen light.

"What does it say?" Eshe asked, craning her neck to try and see without crossing the circles.

Dinah frowned at the glyphs hammered into the lead tablet.

"Not a clue."

"But it's uncast now," said Isolde. Her face was carefully blank but a little kink at the corner of her mouth showed that she was puzzled.

Dinah turned pale. "If Charlie's carrying one of these as well, could he allow something passage through the wards at Kallin Beck?"

"Powerful as they are, yes. Even your cottage has to play by the old accords," Isolde said.

"What kind of agreement has loopholes that huge?" Eshe asked, dusting a gap through the first protective circle.

Isolde looked from Eshe to Dinah.

"She's new," Dinah said, to which Isolde gave a quiet hum.

"So, we're thinking there's more than one of these things?" Eshe asked, giving the potato sack a poke.

Dinah was on her feet, breaking the inner circle.

"We can't risk it."

She reached out to take the uncast defixio, but so did Isolde. Their hands crossed as if they were playing snap. After a moment, Isolde conceded, and Dinah put it in her pocket along with the bronze pin.

With a sack full of nightmare slung over Eshe's shoulder, she and Dinah ran out into the night.

Not quite believing the fruit that her bad luck had yielded, and unable to hold back her wry smile, Isolde followed.

CHAPTER THIRTEEN

Dinah's boots hammered the cobbles, the road, then the old dirt track as she ran all the way home on what felt like a single breath.

Kallin Beck cottage was in darkness when they arrived. With their safety sworn to them, Dinah's friends would be trying to get some sleep. Why wouldn't they? But now she knew more, she knew that their safety wasn't so certain. If they had only caught Meredith's nightmare then Charlie's could be inside already. Or maybe it had been and gone, and Theo was about to wake to find his husband dead beside him.

Kallin Beck had always been safe, impenetrable. She'd never been told of a single instance where something had breached the enchantments. Whatever they were dealing with was far above her supernatural pay grade. It was cunning, and she had only one witch in denial, and another who was potentially an enemy, to back her up.

Dinah felt her fingers had barely brushed the door handle, but it flew open under her hand. The house was pitch black and still as only country houses can be at night. She stood on the threshold, willing her hammering pulse and rasping breath to be quiet so that she could hear anything inside the house. Nothing. No movement. Pushing out her concentration, she reached for the scent of sawdust, the taste of custard, or the feeling of wool gloves on her hands, the sensations of her friends.

They were there alright, but so was that rising, deafening pressure in Dinah's ears. The nightmare was already inside. She knew the cottage well enough to navigate in the dark, but Eshe was slower and stumbling, and Isolde faltered at the threshold as any sensible witch might.

Down the short hall beside the stairs Dinah moved with purpose, dipping her hand into the mason jar. Halting in the living room doorway, she blew the dust into the space like a glittering kiss, and moved quickly on when no nightmare appeared. Into the kitchen she blew another handful and found nothing. Her approach wasn't efficient, she knew. The impish creature could hide from the revealing dredge in some high corner, under a table, or behind a curtain. But she had to try something and that was her only idea. Finally, she reached the room she'd been dreading, the room where her friends might be lying drained and dead.

Instead, she found a curious scene. Theo sat

against one wall, legs spread across the protection circle's lines, stroking Charlie's head in his lap. Charlie was snoring, a safe sound which instantly set Dinah at ease. Meredith stood by the old pine sideboard, staring at the doors which were strapped closed with a curtain tieback. It took Dinah a moment to realise what her friend was holding: the leg of one of the dining chairs. As Dinah dashed in, her handful of homemade magic ready to go, Meredith turned to her.

"Sorry, D. We broke your chair."

At the sound of her voice, Theo jumped, and Charlie jerked awake, startled and fretful. They settled quickly when they spotted Dinah, with Eshe now caught up and peeking in over her shoulder.

The sideboard rattled, and a low growl escaped from between its doors.

"There's something in the cupboard," Meredith said by way of explanation.

"A nightmare," Dinah replied.

"Yeah, it was a bit," Meredith replied earnestly.

"No, it's called a nightmare. We got one too," Eshe cut in, brandishing her potato sack.

Meredith nodded as if she understood.

Against her better judgement, Isolde poked at the cottage's threshold with the toe of her boot. When she wasn't thrown back across the garden, she extended a hand and passed right through the doorway unhindered. She could hear the others chattering, and see lamps being lit down the hallway, so she took a moment to look around. Both on the door jamb and the stonework around it, on the corner of a flagstone on the floor, and in the eaves above, she spotted apotropaic marks hidden and brazen, new, old, and ancient. No wonder the place had knocked her on her butt. If these were the witch marks that she could see, she couldn't imagine what enchantments might lie underneath. Her mother was right to be fretful of this place. With a couple of witches inside it was a pleasant little home, free from supernatural assault, but if something darker took up residence it would be an impenetrable fortress. Something that knew old magic and ways around infallible rules that witches relied upon, like thresholds.

Rubbing the backs of her arms to fight the cold shiver that ran through her, Isolde followed the sound of voices. The dining room was very much as she had seen when peeking in earlier that night, but now she could see the protection circle on the floor, the smashed furniture from the recent scuffle, and she realised that the spare people weren't other witches at all, but victims of the nightmares.

"New girl?" one of them said, and it was aimed at her. It was the librarian that she had run out on earlier that day. *That must be Charlie,* she surmised.

Eshe and Dinah looked between them.

Theo's eyebrow arched. He looked drained. Watching over Charlie had exhausted him. "Friend of yours?" he said.

"Yes," replied Dinah.

But Eshe said at the exact same time, "Remains to be seen."

Isolde tried to ignore that as Dinah made swift introductions. "And she's helping us with the nightmares, aren't you, Isolde?"

"So far, no," Isolde admitted. "We should find the other defixio."

The three non-magical folk exchanged blank glances, but pockets were checked and soon a second lead scroll was dug from the lining of Charlie's parka hood.

"How did that get in there?" the librarian asked.

"Cleverly," Isolde muttered.

"Someone clearly has something against Meredith, Charlie, and Sarah," Eshe said. "But who could you all have annoyed enough for murder?"

Five throats swallowed hard. Isolde scanned the collective faces for ticks and tells, lies and spells.

"We're tired," Dinah said. "And for now, we're safe again. We should rest if we can and figure this out in the morning. But first, tea and a snack."

As Dinah removed herself to boil the kettle and gather homemade cookies onto a chipped old plate, Eshe revealed the second struggling nightmare and bagged it with the first, then stowed them both back inside the dining room cabinet. The rest of the group made small talk, dancing around the idea that there could be a murderer on their trails.

"Always belly first with Dinah, isn't it?" Meredith chuckled but there was no real joy in it.

"I appreciate anyone who knows where her next cuppa is coming from," Theo replied.

Isolde looked between them all. They had no idea. To them Dinah was just a tea-belly with baking on the brain. But Isolde knew better. She knew that magic of any kind took a toll on the mortal body, and that hot drinks and sweet treats were the perfect way to replenish magical reserves. She, for one, was looking forward to a snack after the evening's spells and hex-breaking had left her feeling weak at the knees. But apparently these people didn't know that - even Eshe who seemed so knowledgeable about some aspects of the supernatural seemed ignorant of the fundamentals.

Dinah returned and they all ate and drank in relative silence.

"I'll keep watch while you all sleep," Isolde said, apropos of nothing. She knew it was offered too readily, too obviously, and she bit the inside of her mouth to hide her disappointment in herself.

"We'll do it together," Eshe replied with a large dose of scepticism.

Bedrooms and blankets were handed out. The house turned quiet apart from the creak of floorboards and settling of stone. Eshe took up her post in one of the living room's comfortable chairs and Isolde sat in the furthest corner of the sagging sofa. Only the soft glow of a table lamp spoke to the existence of life inside the old cottage.

Isolde sat in the low gloom of the cottage that had been so recently forbidden to her. She had made it, by no cunning of her own but by luck. She would take it, but it made the victory a little hollow. A few times she looked over to Eshe and found the student already looking back. Isolde snapped her head away and casually glanced around the room. Every movement felt robotic and forced under Eshe's gaze, like she'd forgotten how to just be. Her mind drifted back to her solitary little camp, cold and direly basic but at least she wasn't being watched. After a while she risked another glance toward Eshe and found the student's head resting against the chair's winged back in sleep. Tension poured out of Isolde's body. She could almost feel it - from the tips of her ears to her toes. Now was the time to get what she'd needed all along.

First, she wiggled her toes. The snack and hot tea had done its job, and she felt her reconnection to her magic coming up through her boot heels. Stretching out her balled fists, she felt her concentration expand into the room until it touched every stone wall, the thick old curtains, the patchy rug over the flagstones. Only the iron fittings of the fireplace pushed back. Now that she was inside, she could feel the individual witch marks, enchantments and blessings that studded the cottage from foundation to chimney top. There were hundreds, all glowing with different shades of intent, all bestowed on this one place by different people in different times. The effect was like a magical graffiti wall and so many of the marks Isolde couldn't even recognise. There were new forms, new shapes, some scarred into stone and others painted on with blood or lipstick, faded by weather but with the intent bestowed by the mark still strong. There were braids of hair in handsewn spirals hidden in the mortar, even an indecipherable sigil on the underside of the flagstone at her feet.

Isolde brought in her focus and took a deep, steadying breath. Just before she came fully back to herself, she thought she felt something at the edge of her perception: pride, faint but undeniably smug.

"Hecate, protect me," she muttered. She checked to see whether she had woken Eshe, but the student slept on. She whispered, "House? Can you hear me?"

Nothing. Obviously. What had she expected? The sensation had been so faint, so fleeting, but it had been there. That was all she needed to know. It was more than she had wanted to know. With every second that she stayed in the cottage she found her mother's words coming back to her:

"Two witches are as good as no witches at all."

Perhaps, in this case, she was right. Isolde had been thinking about it all wrong, thinking that the cottage was there to protect its inhabitants. But it should have a coven to protect it in return.

Checking again that Eshe was still asleep, Isolde eased herself to standing, in case the old sofa creaked, and headed for the living room door. She'd spotted the bookcase in the dining room and had been itching to browse ever since. A house like this had to have some rare old texts for her to read.

"Where are you off to?"

Isolde jumped, making a noise as if she'd stubbed her toe. Eshe's eyes were open and on her, even though she hadn't moved from her old position.

"I'm checking on the nightmares," Isolde said.

"I think we'd know if they'd escaped."

"I'd rather not give them the chance."

Eshe humphed, pushed herself up to sitting and readjusted her blanket over her knees. "Are you ready to tell me why you were following us? Dinah might have forgotten in all the rushing around, but I haven't."

Isolde sighed, leaning on the doorway with her arms folded. Her shoulders were up by her ears again, she noticed. She was back on guard, and she hated how easily she had slipped into it. How nice would the Kallin Beck witches, or anyone, have to be before that wasn't her first reaction?

"I'm researching the cottage," she said. "You might not know how powerful this place is, but it's special. More special than any of you realise."

Eshe was nodding. "A lot of witches have come

here for a very long time, every one leaving a blessing behind."

Isolde's eyebrows lifted in surprise. "You know?"

"I'm here to study it too." Eshe offered. "For my Masters in Folklore. I'm mapping the apotropaic marks and what they might mean to the development of folklore, the sharing of beliefs across places and in different times. I'm starting to think that Kallin Beck might be a place of pilgrimage, and a place of teaching. Every witch who came here would leave her mark and learn the marks of others, taking them away with them. That's how witches' marks can appear so far apart but be so similar. At least, their underpinning principles often are. That's my working theory. But I wasn't expecting marks from all over the world, and from so far back in time. I think some of the stones might have been brought from other places, you know? With the marks already intact?"

"You came for fairy tales and found real magic."

Eshe laughed. "Yeah, something like that. I could have done without it, to be honest. I've got a dissertation to write."

In the gloom, a smile crept onto Isolde's lips.

"So that's all it was? Curiosity?" Eshe prodded again.

"Yes," Isolde lied. And then she told the truth. "I didn't expect you to be so welcoming. Or that you'd let another witch in. I thought you'd be more - territorial."

"Dinah has a way of letting people in that can catch you off guard." Eshe looked Isolde right in the eye. "And I'd hate for anyone to betray that trust. She doesn't deserve that."

Something about that made Isolde shudder. Yes,

she was just a guest. The cottage had let her in, let her peek at it. And for all she wanted to peel back every layer of magic to see how the place ticked, she would never be so disrespectful. Not even her mother's orders could make her do that.

In that moment, Isolde sensed the sun peering over the dales, testing the new day, and she changed her mind about poking any further. For now.

"It's morning. You should all be alright now," she said. "I should go."

"You don't have to," Eshe replied, a little too coldly.

"I do." Isolde moved toward the door and paused. Maybe it was the fresh dawn, or the realisations of the last few minutes, and maybe being alone in the woods had let a kernel of loneliness into her heart that she had been trying to ignore. Whatever it was, she said: "I- might come back."

"You'll be welcome," Eshe said.

Isolde slipped out of Kallin Beck, making sure to click the door quietly closed behind her.

Chapter Fourteen

Dinah lay staring at the ceiling, her duvet up under her chin like a sickly Victorian child, and waited for dawn. She wanted to rest so badly, to just close her eyes, but every time she did, Sarah's foot sticking out from under her blankets came back to her. That first sign that she'd failed, that she'd been too slow, too stupid to see the danger. She wished desperately, and for the thousandth time, that her mum was there. Not just for comfort, but because if she had been then Sarah would still be alive.

Her eyes burned, and her throat was tight but there were no tears. When the first glow of sunlight came over the horizon, she wondered if she'd blinked all night. She got up, dressed, and headed downstairs.

The house was silent, like it had been in the old

days before Eshe had arrived, when there was only Dinah rattling around the stone and stained wood, but she knew that she wasn't alone. Even while they slept, her knack had still picked up the faint sensations of her friends. The taste of liquorice was gone though. Isolde had left some time in the night, which wasn't a big surprise, but Dinah mused that it was a shame.

Into the dining room she went and, creeping closer to the sideboard cupboard, she felt no pressure change from the nightmares either. Confident in her knack, she untethered the handles and found just an empty sack inside. The dawn had pushed the creatures back to wherever they came from. She hoped that with the defixiones taken care of, they wouldn't return. Still, a threat hung in the air. Someone had put those ancient curse tablets in place. Someone wanted to get rid of Dinah's friends.

With that thought rattling around her head, Dinah retreated to the sanctity of her kitchen. The next step was hidden from her, like a morning fog rolling in over the dales, but she had to do something with her hands, and so she baked. By the time Eshe woke and came into the kitchen, blanket wrapped around her shoulders and her glasses still in the top pocket of her knitted vest, there were fresh scones and a loaf of bread on the kitchen island. Waiting for those to cool, Dinah had found a group of mismatched glass jars and was adding in pinches of powder and sprigs of herbs.

Eshe watched for a while, her back to the kitchen wall.

"You can help, if you'd like," Dinah said. "You can draw a protective sigil on each lid for me. Then your mark will be sealed inside with my herbs —"

"No," Eshe said, a little too sharply before she softened it. "I don't think I can. Sorry, Dinah. Yesterday was- you know. And I don't think I really knew what I was getting into. I still thought that it might all be in your imagination, like this whole town has some mass hysteria going on. Lovely, lovely people but all a bit eccentric. I thought I'd just play along, and it would all come out alright once we'd played out looking for this invisible thing. Then you'd realise that Sarah was just a terrible, terrible, freak accident, that there was nothing that anyone could have done. And then I'd be here to look after you, and help you feel better, because you're my friend. I really do mean that. I think you're brilliant. But I wasn't expecting that thing to be real."

Dinah stopped what she was doing to listen, her soft brown eyes bathing her friend with understanding.

"You were so brave, you know," she said. "You say that you didn't expect it to be real, but I didn't expect you to believe it either. I never wanted to really get you dragged into this stuff. I always thought you'd just head home when you were done here, and you could tell stories of the crazy lady you once stayed with on the dales."

Eshe was shaking her head. "There's no way I'd do that. Even if I do have to go home sometime. I'm not leaving you forever, Dinah. Come here." Eshe crossed the kitchen, arms open, and she folded Dinah into them. "You really thought I was going to leave you? This place - even with the insanity and really real monsters - it's the best place I've ever been. You're the best person I've ever met."

Her face buried in Eshe's knitted vest, Dinah's voice came out muffled. "Oh, give up."

"No, you give up," Eshe chuckled. "I'm not leaving but- I don't know if I can do this magic thing. Do I sound like a child if I say that I'm scared?"

Dinah pushed back from her friend so that she could look up at her. "I'm bloody petrified."

They both laughed and re-engaged the hug.

"Eshe, I think you're brilliant too. And you don't have to get involved. But I do."

"I know."

"And for what it's worth, I think you're already a brilliant witch. I couldn't have done any of that stuff without you last night. I don't know any of the stuff that you know, even if you thought it was all make believe."

Eshe eyed the glass jars on the countertop. "What would you want me to do with those?"

"No, it's ok. They'll work just fine without a sigil," Dinah said. She sniffed, produced a handkerchief from her sleeve like a magician, and wiped her nose.

"I want to," Eshe said. "This time, at least. I want to make sure everyone is as safe as they can be."

Dinah held her friend's hand. "I'll believe in you, if you believe in me," she said.

Eshe smiled, and her face turned determined as she looked down at the stack of jar lids, grabbed a stick of charcoal that Dinah kept around, and cast her mind back over her studies.

Signs and sigils danced inside her head. There were so many, so many different ways that ancient logic became magic. So many names of gods and spirits, some contradicting or overlapping each other. How was she supposed to choose the right ones?

"Intent is what counts," Dinah added as if she could read her friend's mind. Grabbing a carafe of vinegar with a cork lid, she added a slosh to each jar. "And make it your own. Your witch mark. An Eshe original."

In Japan it matters what order the strokes are made, Eshe thought. Maybe she could layer the imagery of her sigil using the order of her strokes.

She drew a lazy, diagonal S for the curve of Kallin Beck as it snaked through the dales and down past the cottage. She felt safe here, with Dinah, and so her intent went into making the bearers of these jars as safe as she felt. Then she began to draw small upward branches from that gentle snake until she had a rudimentary antler. One of the oldest gods of the British Isles was a stag-horned figure with many names, and she evoked that ancient protective spirit of nature next. Then, at the bottom end of the antler, she drew an oval spiral like a fingerprint, to represent herself. Looking at the sigil, simple and a little wonky, Eshe smiled. It had place, it had power, and it had a little piece of her.

Dinah's eyes flicked over to the sigil and then back to her work. She smiled ever so slightly so as not to make Eshe feel self-conscious.

"I like it," was all she said.

Eshe drew more on the underside of the jar lids before screwing them in place, then Dinah gift wrapped them with string, having Eshe place her finger to hold the knot.

"And there we go. Our first binding together," Dinah said, holding up the jar.

"Do you think it will work?"

Dinah hesitated ever so slightly before she said,

"Absolutely."

One by one the others woke up and came downstairs. Tea and buttery scones were eaten, and everyone felt rejuvenated. Charlie kept fiddling with his jar of protective mixture. If it got too far away from him as they talked and moved around, he would draw it closer again. Dinah watched him closely. He had been affected by the nightmare far more than Meredith and it was likely to be many nights before he slept soundly again. As for Meredith, anger was overriding her fear.

"We need to find this thing and I'll wrap a chair around its teeth as well," she said. Then apologetically, to Dinah, "But I'll use one of my own next time."

"I'm just glad you could fight the nightmare off."

"We knew something was coming, and it took all three of us —" Theo started.

"And a tieback," added Charlie.

"— and half of Dinah's house, it seems. But we managed."

"I'm just glad that you didn't kill it. That would have been very bad," said Dinah. They all looked at her in silence, waiting for her to go on. "The short version is that there is an old agreement, an accord, between mortals and spirits. We don't hurt them; they don't hurt us. We can banish them back to where they came from, but we can't hurt them. If you'd have killed even a small spirit like the nightmare, something much more powerful might have come to even the score."

A silence strung out between them, weighted with the absence of Sarah.

Dinah added, quietly: "That's how it's supposed to

be."

Meredith humphed. "Well, those nightmares weren't playing by the rules. You said they might have followed us back from camping? But I don't even remember going camping. I've been wracking my brains all night and I just get this feeling that we didn't go. I can remember planning it, I remember packing my rucksack, but I don't remember walking out the door. We had some reason to cancel." She looked at Charlie.

"Yeah," he said.

"You did go," Theo answered. "Because when I got back from my mum's, Charlie's muddy boots were in the hall, his sleeping bag was all tangled up on the floor because he never packs it back up properly —" Theo patted his husband's hand with a loving smile. "—because he's a slob. You went up there, I'm sure of it."

"Then why can't we remember?" Charlie asked, staring down at his jar.

Dinah's jaw was set firm, her teeth grinding as she thought. "Because something happened up there that you had to forget."

Chapter Fifteen

After sleeping in the cottage for a night, Isolde looked at her faithful old tent with what felt like disloyalty. Amabel had bounced her from one side of the country to the other, on one errand after another, and that tent had been with her every step of the way. Crawling into her sleeping bag felt as much like home as anything ever had. And one nap on the sofa of a cottage had left Isolde feeling like a traitor.

"Sorry, tent," she said, and went about packing up her meagre belongings into her ratty backpack.

She'd done her job now. She'd been inside Kallin Beck, she'd taken stock of everything, including the measure of the witches in residence, and that was what her mother wanted. Now, maybe, she'd be allowed to go home to her own bed, if Amabel hadn't turned her room into a storeroom for Vivian's paintings by now.

Or. Or she could not go home. Did she really want to go back to a house that missed her so little? Something itched at the back of her head about the whole nightmare issue. She had the feeling that this was a mortal problem. If some spirit wanted to reach all the way from Sidreal (just one of many but her favourite name for the spirit realm) to the mortal plane and kill someone, they were not only breaking the old accords but would need a damned good reason to do so. The power and cunning that it would take to extend their reach so far, and to avoid repercussions, would be insurmountable. But for a mortal to use nightmares for dire purposes, now that was doable. Yet, somehow far worse. Isolde had done her share of hexing over the years, as ill-advised as it was, but causing spirits to outright murder someone was against the grain of witchcraft at a fundamental level. And more than that, who would want a cafe-owner, librarian, and a bus driver dead so badly? She'd met Meredith and Charlie, and she'd received no bad vibes at all. What could they have possibly done?

None of it made any sense, and that meant there was something she was missing. But she couldn't go back. Pride, perhaps. She was a solitary practitioner and happy that way. Joining a coven, or helping one for a short time, would prove her mother right - and that would be a dire outcome. And it was easier to be responsible for herself alone rather than complicating things. No, she had to investigate without returning to Kallin Beck. Let the kitchen witch and the fledgling sigilist feel safe now that the immediate danger had passed. Isolde, however, had an idea. She was going to speak to the beck itself.

With everything stuffed inside her backpack, and her tent rolled and strapped to the outside, Isolde made for the nearest part of the Beck where it cut through the woods before coming out near to Dinah's cottage. She knew the way from her meditations; how she would find the little silver snake and follow it down to the lake. But this time she was listening for something specific, a hint of a voice in the burbling water.

Shifting her backpack from one shoulder to the other, Isolde finally came across the beck's mossy bank between the trees. The ground was spongy and slippery in places, but she managed to hop from one bank to the other without getting wet feet. Pushing out her concentration, she avoided thinking about all of her internal turmoil by experiencing nature in as present a way as possible. She didn't just wait for the bird to sing and draw her attention, she spotted it before it opened its beak and caught sight of its breath condensing on the air with the shrill note. She let the mossy ground show her where to step, surefooted as a doe. She didn't let a single slosh or ripple of the beck go unnoticed. Every rustle and flap and shuffle of undergrowth tickled and amused her. Although the beck was her focus, when Isolde saw the dilapidated walls of an old sheep shed rising from ivy like grey teeth, she took a diversion. She'd never noticed this in her meditations, proof of what she had always suspected: while magic showed what the naked eye couldn't see, there were some things that could only be discovered with real boots on real ground.

Some poor sheep had met its end in the ruins, and

its bones were piled haphazardly in the ivy choked structure. Isolde looked around, checking for scratches, pawprints, and charring. Nothing. This had happened a long time ago. The bones were old, picked clean, and porous from years of wear. Isolde poked through them, selecting a jawbone, a scapula, and some smaller leg bones and put them in her pack. Then she returned to the beck, washed her hands, and carried on along her way.

With all of the tales of Kallin Beck, and the weight of her mother's obsession, Isolde had expected more from the little stream. She had expected some trickle of power along with the flow, some whisper of consciousness to it, but she felt nothing. Even if the beck didn't want to speak to her personally, she should have still been able to sense the magic. As she reached the treeline where the beck struck out toward Dinah's cottage, Isolde still sensed nothing. Where had these tales of the beck that whispered secrets to the witches who visited come from? Was it all just old tales and, if so, why had the cottage been built there at all? Something didn't add up. Too many things, in fact.

Turning her chin up to regard the sky and closing her eyes, Isolde made her request of the light and became invisible before walking down toward the cottage. She wanted to follow the beck as far as she could, but she really didn't want the Kallin Beck witches to think she had come back to them for some reason. She didn't want them getting used to her being around.

The spell did its job as usual, and Isolde headed down to the back of the cottage. She checked the windows to the kitchen and dining room without really meaning to, but saw no one. The place was quiet. Maybe Eshe and Dinah were out somewhere. Unknowingly, Isolde took a seat on the bank where Eshe liked to take her lunch. Her spell would last a while, and if she was going to hear something from the stream then it would be there.

Setting aside her pack she knelt by the water and reached down, her fingers slipping into the blissfully cool flow. She humphed with interest as her fingers became visible under the water. An odd interaction that she hadn't considered; that the light refracted by the water might confuse the spell. She thought to write it down when she had a chance.

More importantly, as she pushed a little of her intent into the water itself, she came back with nothing that she would recognise as a magical presence. The beck was pretty as it snaked down the slope, past the cottage, and toward the town of Hexford. It reflected the sky in its silver and blue ripples, it made patterns around the many smooth stones that redirected its flow. It was a beautiful, peaceful place. But that's all it was. If there had been magic, there was none now.

Isolde's heart sank. She had so desperately wanted there to be something. She had wanted to converse with the beck's spirit so badly. With a sigh, she got up, dusted off her bottom and knees, and reshouldered her pack. Her hike wasn't done. She would follow the beck all the way to its end. Just in case.

Chapter Sixteen

Everyone had gone home and Kallin Beck felt a little too quiet now. As Dinah sat on the sofa, blankets bundled over her knees and a cup of steaming tea in her hands, staring out of the front window, she missed the tickle of her knack when the others were around. Eshe's fizzing sensation was still there as she was only upstairs in the shower, but Dinah missed Charlie, Meredith, and Theo. While she had lived there on her own, Dinah had never felt sad or lonely. But now that Eshe had lived with her it was as if Dinah and the cottage had grown accustomed to the sensation of someone else running around the house. It was as if it was meant to be filled with life, all those individual dreams and intentions warming up the old stones.

Dinah heard the shower click off above, and the clash of the shower cubicle door. It was that kind of thing that she had come to love. Just hearing her friend go about her business, knowing that she was there, filled Dinah's heart a little.

But what made her run cold was this mystery hanging over them all. Her friends were as safe as she could make them for now. The nightmares had certainly been seen off. But someone had wanted them dead. Someone had taken their memories, and then stolen a friend. Though the apotropaic jars would stop any further supernatural incursions into their homes, fear could now pull away to reveal the grief and hurt that had been hidden underneath. Under the magic, after the battle, there were always the mortal repercussions to deal with.

Dinah thought of her Nana Haigh, or rather the sensation of her. Dinah had been too young when her nan had died to really remember her face, or being read to by her, or walking on the dales with her, but she still had the sensation that her knack had given to her, the feeling of Lavender being crushed between her palms and the scent that was released. Nana Haigh was the only person to ever give Dinah both a sensation and a smell at the same time. It was a good, earthy feeling. Dinah always thought that her nan had given her something immensely powerful in that sensation, not just a connection to her grandparent but to every witch across time who had taken a herb, crushed it between her hands, and used it in their magic to calm and comfort. That was the visceral memory, more than just the colour of her eyes or the sound of her laugh, that her nan had given her. But she also remembered her mother coming home that morning, soaking wet through with her Nana Haigh's spellbook under her arm. Dinah had looked for her nan in her mother's wake, but she hadn't been there. She remembered that her mother's sensation had been absent as well. There was no taste of butter biscuits in Dinah's mouth. It was as if the woman who had returned had lost both her own mother, and herself as well. And Dinah remembered the mortal loss that her mother suffered in the months after, how long the familiar taste had taken to return.

"No one witch can fathom every strand of the web. Nor should they try. Sometimes strands end where we least expect, or split, or fray. And sometimes something unfathomably large breaks the web with a swipe of its finger."

That was her mother's cryptic answer to what had happened the night her nan had died.

Sarah's strand had been broken, Dinah thought. But Meredith, Charlie and Theo's were still there. If only she could see the next strand over, the one that intersected with those of her friends.

Eshe came into the room, bundled in her giant flannelette dressing gown, her hair in a silk scarf, and flopped down into the chair she'd slept in the previous night. It was her favourite reading chair with the perfect balance of light between window and lamp that meant she didn't have to move even if she was reading from midday to midnight.

"I had to wash the last few days off of me," she said.

"It's the magic. It can build up like oil on your skin sometimes," Dinah said without taking her eyes off the window. "You were in the presence of real spells, and real monsters, for the first time, not just my little baking enchantments."

"I know which ones I prefer."

Dinah gave her a weak smile.

"We need to figure out what they've forgotten," she said eventually as if she was halfway through a conversation with herself. "I thought that the amnesia was caused by the nightmares. I wanted Sarah's death to be an accident, too. But there's this gap in the story, the night that they all forgot. What could have happened to cause amnesia like that?"

"Maybe the amnesia was what caused the nightmares to over-eat."

"Maybe."

"What else can we do?"

Dinah made a non-committal sound.

"Your tea's gone cold," Eshe said. Standing, she took the full cup from her friend's hand and retreated to the kitchen to replace it. The kettle was rattling loudly, ready to click, when she turned to find the milk and almost leapt out of her skin. Dinah had appeared in the kitchen doorway.

"The amnesia and the nightmares are the same thing," she said. "We've been thinking about it as if one thing led to the other, as if it's some logical problem. They go camping, see something, get so scared, maybe, that they get amnesia, they come home and the nightmares prey on their affected brains, eating until they kill rather than moving on like they usually would. But why would a nightmare eat from a sick brain? Would you eat an apple with a worm in it?"

Eshe regarded her friend as if she had a worm in her head. "Urm, no."

"Exactly. But what if the amnesia is a spell, Eshe?

Memories can be changed. But they have a nasty habit of leaking out."

"Like in dreams?" Eshe said, drifting across to the kitchen island, spreading her hands on the tabletop. Dinah moved over to meet her.

"Like in dreams!" She was grinning. "But what if you can't dream? No dream, no leak. So, you send a nightmare to each person that you want to keep quiet, which forces them to not have their normal dreams."

"The nightmares were compelled, somehow?"

Dinah nodded deeply, her grin slipping into a grim line. "A second spell. Two spells working in tandem. One deletes the memory and the other makes sure it stays hidden. It just so happens that the combination turned deadly. And then there's the defixiones that make sure the nightmares can get in. Who made them?"

"I- I'd forgotten about them."

Dinah nodded. "In the ruckus, so did I. But someone made them. That's three enchantments working together for a single goal. That's serious spellcraft."

"Why not just kill them? Surely it would have been easier than waiting for a nightmare to do it."

"The old accords. Nothing from the spirit realm can wilfully harm a mortal," Dinah prodded the tabletop. "'Wilfully' is the important part. The nightmares can be considered an unforeseen side effect of a complex, but relatively harmless, spell."

Eshe realised she was gritting her teeth, her jaw felt like iron. "What did they see up there?"

"Something very, very bad that doesn't want to be remembered. We have to find out."

Chapter Seventeen

When she was once more out of sight of Kallin Beck cottage, Isolde let the light, the warmth, and her visibility flood back around her in a shower of frost. The warmth, in particular, was most welcome. As she carried on down the hill to where the beck turned through Hexford, she grabbed an oat bar from her pack to pay back the energy she'd used. As a snack it was fine, but she found herself thinking of, craving, a hot cup of tea and one of Dinah's scones. It was almost a strong enough desire for her to head to The Nook and see whether Meredith had managed to open up. But she bore down on her goal instead and continued to follow the stream as houses started to pop up on either side of it.

The beck widened and became shallower as it

passed through the town. The smooth rocks at its bottom were closely packed like a road in its own right, and it stayed that way as it passed the fjord at Hexford's centre, only getting deeper and wilder again as it passed back out of town. It was lunchtime by the time Isolde reached this part of her journey and the meagre oat bar hadn't done much to fill her up. She had nothing left to eat in her pack, so she let her stomach rumble away, promising herself she would return to town when her little investigation was done.

Still, as she walked, there was no sense of presence in the beck. A glow of enchantment from the town, yes, and a casual observation coming from the cottage, but the stream was only magical in the way that all natural things are.

A copse of trees stood over to one side, from which another small stream joined the beck, and soon other little trickles and dribbles from the dales were pouring in to make the beck stronger, deeper, and faster. When it had become a river in its own right, the beck cut a channel through a rough sand beach and emptied into the lake that Isolde had only ever visited while meditating.

The lake spread out in front of her, encroached upon by trees, tasted by their roots. She enjoyed the shimmering mirror of it, and she remembered the sensation of being held by its murky silt floor. And then she felt what she hadn't while meditating. There was a presence.

Throwing down her pack beside a fallen tree whose topmost branches stretched out across the lake, she sat on the beach, letting the water soak up into her jeans, and dug her fingers down into the wet sand.

The tingle of magic was profound. All natural places held magic, but this was special. The beach, the lake, it held a consciousness. A genius loci. A spirit of place.

In her mind, she called out to it.

"Yes?"

Isolde jerked away from the voice that sounded so clearly beside her. She fell, the wet sand soaking into her shirt and grains peppering her hair.

"Are you quite alright?"

There was an old wooden chair where there hadn't been one before, its legs stuck into the sand so that the seat was ever so slightly tilted backward. In the seat was a young gentleman wearing a regency-style suit in black and silver. His hair was the colour of a moonlight ripple and completely unkempt. His skin was sallow, eyes deep, and mouth thick-lipped and sullen. His trousers were rolled to his thin calves and his feet disappeared into the lake.

"Yes. Yes, I'm fine," Isolde said. "I wasn't expecting —"

"When a witch calls, I answer. That's the polite way of things," the spirit said. He looked out across the lake where there was nothing, not even a duck, to disturb the peace, and gestured to it. "I was hardly busy."

"It's very peaceful," Isolde said with reverence.

"Isn't it just?" the spirit replied.

"I was hoping that I could ask you some questions?"

"Ask away," he nodded to the lake once more and his hair did a strange dance that made it completely realign into a new, wild shape around his head. "Although, as you can see, my realm is fairly small there are quite a few little streams that carry news down into my water."

"It's about the past," Isolde went on.

The spirit turned in its seat but still one foot remained in the water. "Ah, now there I have been."

"Do you have a name?"

"Lots of them. As I'm sure you've heard before. Fossegrim is a favourite. And you are?"

"Isolde Tanner," she replied.

"A Tanner, by jove," Fossegrim said with a chuckle. "A Tanner on my meagre shores."

"You know of us?"

"Oh yes. Many-a Tanner has sat where you sat. Or, you know, over there, and a bit of a ways down there," he pointed out one place after another along the beach. "A Tanner fell in once. Forget her name, now."

"Was it Amabel?" Isolde asked.

"No. No I don't think so."

Isolde swore inwardly. That would have been too spectacular.

But all this informality had made Isolde forget herself and she drew herself up to her feet only to bow almost double again.

"Spirit Fossegrim of this great lake. I come to seek your wisdom —"

"Oh, don't bother with all that," Fossegrim interrupted. "Just ask your question, Isolde Tanner."

"Do you not want a tribute?"

Fossegrim screwed up his face. "I only ever wanted one thing and it isn't something that you can grant. Unless- do you have cake? I haven't had cake in- what year is it?"

"2025."

"A new millennium!" Fossegrim said with what was swiftly becoming a noticeable lack of enthusiasm. "Whoop-dee-doo. Ring the bells. I haven't had cake in a very long time."

"I'm afraid I don't have any. But I could bring some," Isolde offered. "There's a town not too far away."

"A town? Still?"

"Hexford?"

"Yes, I know of it. But perhaps you can bring cake another time. Your question?"

"It's about the beck." Isolde swore that she saw a twitch on the spirit's face, a weirdly mortal thing on an immortal creature. She carried on, watching closely for another. "There are old stories that say the beck was once inhabited by a spirit, one like yourself." The Fossegrim had grown quiet, its muddy grey eyes unblinking as it regarded her. Despite herself, she talked a little faster. "But there's nothing there now."

"Kallin Beck fell silent a long time ago, Isolde." The spirit pointed upward at the gathering dusk. "Even the greater wheels of the heavens have come full circle since then."

"But it could speak?"

"Oh yes. At length, she spoke. Ad nauseam, in fact. What brought you to the beck?"

"It's famous for its predictions."

"Is it now? She's no longer there. But I am longer here. Why not ask me what you would have asked her?"

"Can I?" Isolde asked.

The spirit shrugged.

"And in return? What do you need?" she asked, tentatively.

Fossegrim gave her a wan smile. "Need. Nothing. You don't have to speak to me as you would some faerie trickster. I'm as of the mortal realm as you are, Isolde Tanner. We need no bargains."

Isolde felt her pale skin flush. She should have known that. She could have kicked herself.

"Then, there has been a strange occurrence up on the dales. A group of —" Isolde wracked her brain for an old word for 'camper'. Did people camp whenever the Fossegrim had last spoken to a mortal? "— hikers? Walkers."

Fossegrim nodded in understanding.

"Something happened and they lost their memories. They've been plagued by nightmares. One of them has died. I need to know what happened up there. Who did this to them?"

Silent once more, the spirit was still, his expression glassy. Isolde was reminded how old this thing was, how deep its memory, how patient a genius loci must be, how unlike a mortal mind it's mind must be. "Do you live in Hexford, Isolde Tanner?" he asked, still showing no emotion on his face.

"I'm just visiting."

"Then you should go home, wherever that may be. Tonight, for preference."

Isolde shrank back a little from the reclining spirit. She could feel magic reflexively sparking in her fingertips even though she felt like the threat from Fossegrim wasn't coming from him at all.

"What's going on, spirit?" she asked.

Fossegrim stood, slowly, the lake lapping at his ankles as he took a few steps into the water. He looked out across his little realm, but his eyes were constantly drawn to where the shadows clustered under the trees.

"Someone has come home that has been long away, and it's unlikely that Hexford will survive the reunion."

CHAPTER EIGHTEEN

Thumbing the iron latch, Dinah stepped down into the bakery, leaving Eshe to close the door behind them. She didn't call out for Gabe, she knew too well that he would be up to his elbows in all sorts of things, so she just went around the counter and into the kitchen. She almost bumped into her father coming the other way and he didn't hesitate to grab her into a hug.

"Oh, little one," he said, despite the fact that they were the same height. His moustache tickled her cheek as he spoke. "I heard all about it. Are you alright?"

Dinah didn't speak for a moment, she just settled into his arms and squeezed him right back.

"I'm ok. We're both ok," she said.

Gabe reached out a spare hand to Eshe and squeezed her fingers. Eshe gave him a sad smile and a slight shake of the head. Dinah wasn't really alright at all. The whole thing had hit her hard, and both she and Gabe knew it.

"Cake," Gabe said. "And tea. Immediately."

Always with the cake, always with the tea, Eshe thought with a chuckle. Only now she knew why. Gabe had lived with witches most of his life. He knew the benefits to practitioners of calories and hot drinks. She'd never met Dinah's mother, but she imagined this ritual had started in magic and was now a family tradition. Every time something went wrong, whenever they were depleted down to their lowest ebb, there was tea and cake. Dinah had told her that it was cake that had brought her parents together, after all. Charlotte, when she was still a Haigh, had frequented the bakery, when it had still been run by Gabe's father, for sweet treats after some magic had left her blood sugar low. And Gabe had been there, his moustache still wispy.

Gabe led them through to the kitchen where the heat from the ovens was almost stifling. In a moment, he had provided them with fortifying snacks and tea, and the Kallin Beck witches filled him in on the details that he had yet to hear. He listened with an uncharacteristically grim expression.

"You know that magic isn't my thing, but I've been around your mother long enough to learn a thing or two. For what it's worth, I think you're right. This sounds like a larger problem. Much larger."

Dinah nodded solemnly.

"But who could do spellwork like that?" Eshe asked Gabe.

"It's clever. I'm not sure your mum could do something like that, Dinah. I've never even heard of these defixioes. Sounds a lot like a binding, but the language they used, the lead tablets with the pins, that's serious old-world stuff. Maybe it's a coven, working together." He shrugged to highlight his speculation. "They were up on the hills doing magic that they shouldn't have been, and Mer, Charlie and Sarah saw them. Hexford folk know enough to recognise when something's not right."

"Then why not just kill them?" Eshe asked the question that had been bugging her all along.

"The old accords?" Dinah suggested.

"Or perhaps it was a group of mortals who wanted a spirit to be blamed, to cover their tracks," Gabe offered.

Eshe shook her head. "We're tying ourselves up in knots. We need to apply Occam's Razor. Chances are that they saw something they shouldn't have and someone who doesn't care about these old rules put them under a hex because they couldn't kill them outright for some reason."

"Or they wanted to draw out their deaths," Dinah interjected, staring down into her swiftly cooling tea.

"That's so much worse," Gabe muttered.

"Diabolical," Eshe agreed. "But without more information, we're stumped unless whoever this is does something else."

"No, we can still do something." Dinah set down her tea. "We can get as much information as we can, we can prepare, and we can be vigilant. That's something I wasn't doing before. I should have seen the nightmares for what they were earlier. I won't make that mistake again. I say we go to Hari, we dig into that night and any strange occurrences. Then we go read up. Really read up."

Gabe's eye fell on Dinah in an oddly worried way that Eshe couldn't help but catch. Something passed from father to daughter that looked like sadness.

"But we check the papers first."

"You just want to see Hari," Eshe said, trying to lighten the mood.

Gabe's eyebrows raised and a smile crept under his moustache. "She does, does she?"

"I'm thirty-two years old. Why do you two make me feel like I'm fourteen again?"

"Love will do that to you," Eshe shot back.

"Love?" Gabe added, managing to pile tons of well-natured ribbing into a single word.

"Oh hush, both of you."

The Hexford Gazette building was on the corner of what locals called Artisan Alley. With a curved bay window painted blue and a small, hand painted sign with the name of the newspaper beside the door, it would have been easy to walk right by it. It had been a house, at some point, and so Dinah always felt like she should knock before entering. It was one of the few places in town without any obvious witch marks on the doorframe, their absence far stranger than their presence in a town like Hexford.

Inside was a long wooden counter, which looked more like a bar stolen from some closed down pub. The back room was where the single, huge printer lived, managing the few hundred prints of the paper that were necessary for the area. And the floor above held the archives.

Hari sat behind the counter at his single computer,

typing away. Dinah wondered if he ever got lonely, running the whole outfit by himself. He looked back over his shoulder as they entered, and a pleasant smile stretched across his lips.

His lips. His lips.

Oh, for god's sake, Dinah thought. She inwardly blamed Eshe for poisoning her mind and focussed on Hari's eyes instead.

His large, brown eyes with those lashes like sweeping brushes.

Dinah's self-annoyance came out in a little grunt.

Hari sat back on his squeaky computer chair. "Bad morning?"

Eshe stepped in when Dinah just stood silently, inwardly screaming at the sound she'd made.

"Just had some of Gabe's cakes," Eshe said. "So not as bad as it could be."

"Jealous," Hari muttered in his Bradford accent.

"Well —" Eshe gestured to Dinah who was holding a white cardboard container.

Hari stood up, drifting closer to the counter. Eyes wide, he said, "There's an eclair in there. I can smell it. He knows I love eclairs."

"Just watched him put the cream in, myself," Eshe said.

Hari's eyes narrowed. When he spoke, it was with his gaze fixed on the box in Dinah's hands. "What are you after, that you bring such bribes?"

Eshe looked back to Dinah, who had finally collected herself.

"Information. Maybe a quick swizz on your internet?"

Hari was smiling but it wasn't at the eclair. Eshe watched his face take on a ruddy blush as his eyes met with Dinah's.

Oh, these two, she thought.

After a too-long moment, Hari gestured to the computer. "Swizz away." And then, because this was Hexford, he added, "I'll put the kettle on."

Eshe took point at the keyboard and Dinah hovered behind. When he returned with the tea, Hari perched on the desk and tucked into his eclair.

"Subhanallah," he muttered, and then fell quiet for some time while he finished the whole thing. Finally, collecting the spot of cream from the corner of his mouth, he said, "What are you two looking for? Can I help?"

Eshe didn't answer, her eyes were focussed on the screen that underlit her face.

Dinah cleared her throat. "Last week sometime, we think something weird might have happened on the dales. On the hills over town. It's where Sarah and the others went camping."

Hari nodded. "And by weird you mean?"

Dinah hesitated. "Magical."

"Right, right." There was no judgement on Hari's face. He caught Dinah looking at him with pleasant surprise. "I've been here for almost two years. I've heard enough weird stories to know that the whole town believes in this stuff. I've heard enough people say that you're a witch, and talk about your cottage like it's some sacred place." He shrugged. "Who am I to argue? That's not a journalist's job, far as I'm concerned. I do the reporting, whatever the weirdness may be, and leave judgement to the readers."

"And you've never seen anything yourself while you've been here?" Eshe said, still facing the screen.

"Not a damned thing. I don't think the ghosts and

ghoulies like me."

"Good," blurted Dinah, and then clapped her mouth shut.

Hari looked curious.

"I just mean that it means the town is safe. If bad things are staying away," explained Dinah.

"And that you're — I mean, everyone is safe," Eshe added, purposefully clumsy.

A little smile crept onto Hari's face and he changed the subject. "So, what have you found, Eshe?"

"Nothing, yet."

"It could just be that I didn't hear about it. I'm only one man, after all. And all the bake sales, charity events, and giant vegetables that people grow around here keep me busy." There was a hint of annoyance under his humour. It was easy to see how a Bradford journalist could be bored to tears in a place like Hexford.

Not for the first time, Dinah wondered why Hari was there at all.

"Hit the bookmarks at the top there, Eshe. I've got the regional news pages saved."

They flicked through the last week's papers, looking for anything that rang bells, but found nothing.

"Try the dales newspaper archive? It's the national park area paper," Hari added.

Scrolling through pages and pages of tiny articles with flashing clickbait borders had Eshe's eyes burning.

"Give me a well-referenced reading list, any day. How do you find anything in all this?" she sighed.

"I just kind of sit and read everything, every

week." Hari shrugged. "It's not super surprising that you're not finding anything. Hit that folder for me, Eshe? It's something I've been working on in my spare time." He looked sheepish. He gestured to a folder marked 'Historic mentions of Hexford'. "Maybe for a book or something, I don't know yet."

Dinah couldn't help a little smile creeping across her lips. He wanted to write a book. She thought that was the most attractive thing she'd ever heard come out of his mouth. Or anyone's.

"There's nothing in it," Eshe said.

"That's my point. No mentions of Hexford. All the way back to the Domesday Book."

Dinah swallowed. She could feel a conversation coming. One that she'd been putting off. She crept a step backward, away from the oncoming question. But Eshe and Hari were already turning slowly in their seats. She was caught in the crossfire of their eyes.

"It's a long story," she said.

Hari's eyes did that narrowing thing again. "My favourite kind."

"I don't even know if it's true."

"Subjective," Eshe cut in.

"Will you stop looking at me like that, the both of you?" she hugged her mug with both hands, staring down into the swirling beige. "The town isn't on the maps because Kallin Beck hides it. It's part of the enchantments. There's always been witches here and the enchantment started just at the cottage then got bigger and bigger as more witches added to it, and now Hexford is kind of- not really where everything else is, most of the time."

"It's a sanctuary," Eshe said. "I knew it. When

were you going to tell me?"

"You seemed so excited to figure it all out yourself. So, I kept quiet."

"Are you telling me that everyone who lives here is a witch?" Hari said.

"No, no. Of course not. Kallin Beck is the only place where witches still live. But if their family has been here long enough, their ancestors definitely were. Or they were something else."

"Please don't elaborate. I think I'm about to have a breakdown," Hari said.

Eshe leaned out of the chair to take Dinah's hand. "Breakdown be damned. Tell us everything."

"That's the important bits. If you're a bit magical you can usually find a safe place to stay in Hexford, if you need it. No one asks too many questions, no one judges, and it's very likely that no one will find you either."

"But if they do?" Eshe pushed.

"Then the witches at Kallin Beck are here. Whoever they might be at the time. It hasn't always been my family. Nana Haigh moved in when she was a girl. She lived in Retford before that, I think."

"I'm not magical at all. What about me?" asked Hari.

Dinah shrugged and gave him an apologetic smile. "No one's perfect."

"Hmph. Well, that's stumped us as regards the newspapers." Eshe turned back to the computer, eyeing it as if it had finally let her down after so many years of study. "Is there anything else we could check, Hari? Anything at all?"

"There's the event calendar, I guess. It highlights upcoming special interest stories like anniversaries, national days, things like that. But that's all I've got."

Dinah leaned in. "We should check the moon phase as well, if there's a worship day for any religion or culture. Pagan feasts, maybe? Although it's none of the biggies, obviously."

Hari leaned over Eshe's other shoulder so that he could reach the mouse, and now all three of them joined in the research like an underlit research Cerberus.

"Here. Moon phase was gibbous. Is that good?" Hari asked, looking at Dinah who didn't seem particularly fazed as she scanned the page and pointed to a stock photo of a long trailing comet.

"There."

Eshe started to read. "'A rare occurrence will visit our skies this week. Houghton-Ensor is a long period comet crossing paths with earth once every 302 years. Its rarity makes for an exciting opportunity for comet chasers, astronomers, and even astrologists.' It gets a bit click-baity after that, just repeating itself."

"Three hundred years," Dinah said under her breath, eyeing the stock photo attached to the article. "Some people might find significance in that. The kind that would want to be up on the dales where there's less light pollution. The kind that might not want people to see what they were up to, the kind for whom dark spellwork might be perfectly reasonable."

All three heads exchanged worried glances.

Chapter Nineteen

If Isolde wanted to actually go home and not just visit by astral projection, it would take time to get there. The Tanner family home was west, toward the Pennines. But first she needed to get far enough away from Hexford that she could find one of the bus routes that entirely bypassed the veiled village every day. She followed the road out of Hexford, which faded into a dirt track after a while, then became nothing but a shale path before meeting an intersecting tarmac road. She looked back over her shoulder at what appeared to be nothing more than a sheep path, and marvelled at how she had managed to find it the first time around. It had taken every divination method she knew, and quite a few rumours from big city covens, until the swing of a confused pendulum had made her realise that its uncertainty meant that she wasn't lost, but instead was close - the movement like a compass spinning on the north pole.

She walked a little way down the grass verge to the same bus stop that she had arrived at days ago. There she waited until only a kiss of light remained of the sunset. The dales became dark slowly, the light slipping back from the many valleys and crevices as if the hills were filling up with shadows. Soon Isolde was standing in the pitch black with only the moon and a few cloud-shy stars giving off any light. Night was no big problem for her. Alone was no big problem either. She had three athames scattered on her person that she wasn't shy about using if need be, but the truth was that she'd never felt the need. Midnight graveyards, monolithic ritual sites and rarely-trodden roads filled her with peace. There was something about silence, the weight of stone, the enduring strength of death that just made her feel at home. Of course, her mother thought she was mad. Then again, Amabel didn't often mix with other people either, so there was hypocrisy at work.

Still, waiting for the last bus to take her away from Hexford, Isolde found herself looking over her shoulder. Something about what the spirit Fossegrim had said gave her pause. Hexford was as protected as anywhere she had ever known, Kallin Beck was damned near impenetrable, but Fossegrim had been so certain that someone - he had said someone - was coming that the town should fear.

Knowing what she did about Kallin Beck and its witches, Isolde thought it best to leave. Not to run away, as Fossegrim suggested, but because she was certain that there was nothing useful to be found in the little village or the cottage itself. Dinah and Eshe certainly wouldn't know what was coming. No, Isolde had to go home where she knew there were books and even some scrolls, where her sister Lucia spent her time painstakingly preserving and copying out old manuscripts before they were lost to the moths. She would know something. Perhaps Amabel herself would grace Isolde with some advice rather than orders.

Isolde snorted out loud in the dark. That wouldn't happen. She was arriving unannounced to a home that her mother had kept her from for over a year. She wasn't welcome. It would be a flying visit. Maybe she could get in to see her sisters and back out without even bumping into her mother. She twiddled with the Hecate charm on her bracelet for luck.

Out of the dark like a luminescent caterpillar, the bus appeared and disappeared over subsequent hills until it hissed to a halt in front of her. As the doors opened, the bus driver regarded Isolde with wonder. It was the same middle-aged man who had dropped her off on the remote spot just a few days before. She couldn't tell from his expression whether he was surprised to see her again, or whether he was petrified to be picking up a pale and black clad young woman on a pitch-dark road in an otherwise empty bus.

He said nothing, just watching as Isolde climbed aboard, dropped a pound coin in the little tray by his elbow and sat down a few rows behind him. The bus rattled and set off, but in the rearview mirror Isolde could see the driver kept looking back at her. Perhaps every time he was surprised that she hadn't just disappeared. She couldn't help but smile at the thought of being mistaken for a white lady haunting the Yorkshire dales.

The bus rumbled through the dark like some glowing bug in a vast underground cave, the stars above like the twinkling dew of stalactites. Isolde found her head resting against the cool window as the rocking of the bus lulled her into a state of peace. She found her mind wandering back to the lake. Not in meditation, just in thought. She wondered what the spirit Fossegrim did on his own out there. Did spirits feel loneliness or boredom? Surely not. They were timeless, and such things didn't make any sense or every immortal spirit in the world would have been stark raving bonkers. But Fossegrim wasn't bonkers. He was pragmatic, and a little playful. She liked his voice. And how his hair was a climbing silver wave. She liked his grey eyes. They reminded her of the silt she had sunk into at the bottom of the lake in her meditations, how it had taken her weight entirely, how pretty the dank light had been filtering from above. How at peace she had been in the arms of those depths.

Isolde's eyes snapped open from where they had been half closed. She sat dead upright on the bus seat.

"Stop it, you fool," she muttered to herself. "Stopitstopitstopit."

The bus driver checked his mirror again, his brow knotted at the pale young woman talking to herself.

Chapter Twenty

There was a chill in the air that cut right through Dinah's cardigan as she and Eshe waited for Hari. He came out of the Gazette building zipping up his jacket. Dinah watched his hands as they slid into his pockets to search for his keys. Her hands bunched against the cold.

"So, what now?" Hari asked as he fought with the door which always stuck in the jamb.

"Oh, um. The next part we kind of have to do on our own," Dinah answered.

Hari nodded, his lips tight. "Witchy business. I see. Sodding door."

"It's just- dangerous."

Eshe butted in. "I've already seen some stuff I'd rather not have."

"Right, right. Well mi internet es su internet." Hari paused for a breath before yanking the door one last time. "Let me know how it goes, I guess?"

He gave them an awkward little nod-and-smile combo and the witches left him to tackle the Gazette door.

"Couldn't we have used him? He's smart, Dinah."

"Yeah. But… you know."

"Mhm." Eshe said with a sly smile.

Taking her friend's elbow, Dinah headed for the high street. By the time they'd crossed the street and were passing the darkened bay windows of The Nook, they heard Charlie calling to them from behind. He was hurrying along with Hari.

"Oh, thank God. Gabe said you were at the Gazette, but I thought I'd missed you," he said. "Me and Mer had weird dreams last night. The exact same dream."

Dinah and Eshe looked at Hari who stood to one side, hands deep in his coat pockets. "Don't mind me. Just a normie on the sidelines, here. I'm not even listening, really."

"Where's Mer?" Dinah asked.

"She's waiting in the library while I came to find you."

"Ok. Let's go get her."

They started to walk away. Only Eshe looked back to see Hari slowly turning back the way he'd come, his purpose served now that he had delivered Charlie. She thought for a moment.

"Oy," she said, making him turn back. "Where are you going?"

He pointed down the street, presumably toward home.

"Wrong way. You're with us."

One by one they filed into the community library, Dinah giving Hari a slightly surprised look but not commenting as Eshe ushered him inside. Meredith was sitting at one of the computers, staring into the screen like an addict.

"I hope you know what's going on, Dinah. Because I can't find a damned thing," Meredith said.

Charlie muttered something about putting the kettle on and disappeared for a moment with Eshe. The rest of the group sat at one of the large communal tables.

Hari investigated the uncomfortable chairs and muttered to himself. "I've not sat in one of these since school. Always thought they were designed for torture."

"These dreams, D," Meredith started. "I thought the nightmares were bad but something about these dreams is so much worse."

The tea tray returned and soon all five of them were sitting around the table hugging their mugs.

"It's not even the images," Charlie said, checking with Meredith. "It's the feeling. It scares me."

"But you don't seem affected like with the nightmares." Eshe said. "You're not drained and all grey-looking like you were."

"No, this is definitely different," Meredith replied.

"Maybe just start at the beginning then," said Dinah. "As much as you can remember."

Meredith exchanged glances with Charlie before starting to talk. The whole ordeal had left them exhausted. Haunted. Both sat a little hunched, their voices were a little low, as if someone might overhear what they were describing.

"We're at the camp. The fire's going really well and we're just sitting around chatting. Sarah's there." Meredith paused. "But it gets dark fast. Like the last light goes out of the sky really fast."

"And even though we're on the dales it's like- like we're surrounded by trees. Or the shadows of trees but without the actual trees. That doesn't make sense, does it?" Charlie cut in.

"Yeah, like the shadows kind of build up like they do in the woods until we can't really see the stars properly. There's just the moon —"

"And the shadows keep coming."

"— and they keep coming until even the fire is dim and feels far away even though I'm sitting right next to it. I'm freezing cold and I know that Charlie and Sarah are saying something, but I can't make out what."

"It's just like I can hear the panic in their voices but not the words."

Meredith nodded. "And then we all look up, like we don't have a choice, and the stars are so faint, but there's this comet streaking silver and white across the sky and it's so bright that it burns. I try to look away —"

"We all do."

"— but we can't. And then the comet's gone again but there's something still there with us. He's sitting by the fire."

Dinah interrupted where she'd been stunned into silence before. "He?"

"Oh yeah," Charlie said under his breath. His eyes were fixed on his steaming mug as if it was the saddest thing he'd ever seen. "It's him, alright. He says something that feels like an apology. But I can't make out the words."

Meredith shook her head quietly. She didn't know either.

Eshe leaned forward, concentrating on Charlie's quiet voice. "And then?"

"Then he gets up and walks away. Just like that. And I have this feeling —" Meredith said. She looked at Charlie, but Charlie wouldn't meet her eye. "I look up and I'm damned certain that it's the last full moon we'll ever see."

"Dread. That's the word," Charlie said, his voice fading even further so that the others had to strain to hear. "It's like knowing that a monster's been let into the school yard, and we're trapped inside, just watching through the window."

CHAPTER TWENTY-ONE

The first bus took Isolde in the wrong direction for a while, to Knaresborough where she could change to head back north again. Stepping down to the street from the bus, she could instantly feel the old magic that lingered along the shores of the River Nidd. The bus driver clicked his sign to 'Out Of Service' and pulled away, leaving Isolde with only the flickering glow of the bus station's awnings for light. The streets around her were in darkness. Not a single window was lit. She checked the sky and saw that the moon was on its way down to the horizon. Not too long until daylight. So, she slept under the bus station's glass awning with a little magic pushed into her backpack so that it radiated warmth as she hugged it to her chest. She was hungry again, and she hadn't had anything to drink for a long while, and so the magic didn't last all the way until morning. But she was used to waking up to a chill.

Knaresborough was a Yorkshire town and so the cafes opened early. The nearest in sight of the bus station was a chain cafe with overpriced offerings, but as soon as the sign flicked to open, Isolde was inside, almost startling the young lad who was on the early shift.

"Tea, please," she said and, eyeing the pre-packed sandwiches, she ordered a sausage roll too.

Thankfully, her card made a happy beep when she tapped it. Her mother always put a little money into her account for essentials, but it was never enough that Isolde could afford to be spontaneous with where or what she would eat.

The cafe was no Nook, and the sausage roll was pretty much tasteless after Hexford's baking, but it went down alright. Isolde left the teabag in her cup while she drank so that the last sips were basically soup. She took her time, soaking up the warmth from the cafe's heating. Transit vans visited with workers in hi-vis vests destined for labour sites all over the area. The postman came and went. An old man with a ragged dog read the paper at a nearby table. Isolde kept her eye out of the cafe window, watching the different lives wheel about. A thin rain started to fall, and she had to keep wiping the condensation from the window. When her next bus came in, she put a little magic into her boots to hold in the warmth that she had collected, and headed out.

What mighty works I weave, she thought.

What a powerful witch she was, a paragon of the Tanner family famed for their spellcraft and wisdom, using her powers just to stop her toes from dropping off as she trekked from one end of the country to the other.

The next bus was her least favourite although the journey would be blissfully short. From Knaresborough it took the dismal motorway to Darlington. But after an hour or so Isolde would be on another bus, plunging back into the countryside of the North Pennines and a step closer to her family's home. Those buses were older, rickety, slower, but she could at least feel the speed at which she was moving. She still felt connected to the ground rather than racing inches above it.

At an unassuming point along that road, perforated with stop after stop after stop in little villages and one-horse towns, Isolde alighted and found her boots on familiar earth. The final bus pulled away; another driver giving her an odd look. She could feel the pulse of family land under her feet. Now she would have to walk.

There was an easy way, and then there was the way that she liked to go. One way was down a sloping grass valley where you came out higher up than you'd started. The other took Isolde up a rocky crag where stone punched up through patchy grass. Using her hands and feet, she climbed up until she had a healthy sweat about her. Her leather jacket soon went into the pack and as she took the last heave to the top of the crag, the wind caught her full in the face, blowing back her hair and chilling her bare arms under her cut-off t-shirt. Tilting her head back, eyes heavy lidded, Isolde let the wind rock her on her heels dangerously, and actually made a little noise in the back of her throat. Opening her eyes, she took in her homeland, a vista of grey and green where mountain tops held fingers of ancient stone and hidden waterfalls filled the air with a gentle rumble. The Tanner family home might not fill her with joy, but the wilds of the Pennines surely did. They were rough, dangerous. Bones riddled the crannies, and wandering spirits were said to stand on every lane. The Pennines never pretended to be anything but what they were - and anyone with a sound mind took them seriously.

Isolde looked down into the valley, and across the top of the crag she'd climbed. There was a fair way to go, and it would all be on foot. If she wanted to get home before dark, she had to get moving.

"It was a nice moment," she said to herself, and she actually cracked a little smile with no one around to see it.

The crag top led Isolde further from any roads, further from casual eyes. There was nothing up there to draw curious hikers, the ground was too feral for campers. And of course, the ancient Tanners had a little enchantment of their own to turn people aside, should chance bring them that way. Isolde passed a marker on the crag, a witch mark on a protruding rock, that was part of that spell. But to her it was just a signpost that she was close, and she casually pushed her concentration against the enchantment, convincing it that she was an exception to its rule. It yielded.

Rounding the top of the crag, the Tanner family home finally came into view.

Caillehall imposed on the landscape as if it had been dropped from the sky in a single block. On the prominence in the middle of a horseshoe lake of inky water, the mansion stood with its uninspiring stone facade scowling at anyone who managed to approach. The windows reflected the Pennines but gave no hint as to what was inside.

Isolde stood for a moment at a safe distance. She could turn back. No one was expecting her here. Her shoulders sagged and she heaved a sigh. Then, in an effort that was more difficult than any spell she'd ever undertaken, she began the long climb down toward the house.

CHAPTER TWENTY-TWO

Tea went cold in the cups. The sun went down over Hexford, summoning the sweet Night Phlox buds from hiding to flood the streets with their scent once more. On complete autopilot, Charlie brought another pot and let it stew under the knitted cosy.

"I know I'm just some normie scribbler, but the obvious question is what do we do —" Hari snapped his mouth shut when Dinah cut in:

"I don't know."

Eshe looked around the table at the heavy eyes and bunched brows of her friends.

"We'll figure it out," she said but, between her mind and her tongue, her tone changed from positive reinforcement to a question.

None of them noticed the library door swing open

until the figure in the doorway spoke.

"I can help. If you'll admit me."

Meredith's eyes slid upward without her head moving, Charlie's breath caught in his throat. The others either startled or spun in their chairs toward the new arrival.

Backed by an amber streetlight and his face washed out by the library's strip bulbs, the figure was oddly lit, giving him the appearance of an abandoned paper cut-out. With shoulder length hair of dirty blond, and a brow shot through with wrinkles, he seemed on the verge of middle age, perhaps, but he had an open, even friendly face. There was something wrong with his clothes though. They were modern, but they didn't quite gel, as if he'd been designed by a spectacularly untalented window dresser. His jacket was off-white, thigh length and clearly a woman's cut, layered over a green v-neck jumper. His jeans were black, baggy bottomed and frayed, but from out of the cuffs stuck the shiny toes of dress shoes.

"You seem unfettered. Let me introduce myself." With an opening of his hands, he said in a broad Yorkshire accent, "Ule Dagaunet, craving your indulgence."

When no one moved or said anything, the stranger's lips tightened a little and he said, "I presume that my name is new to you. Never the mind."

Eshe turned slowly to Dinah who had both palms pressed to the tabletop, her eyes wide.

Stepping inside, the stranger made slow progress across the library, his hands still open and visible as if in submission, head slightly bowed.

Charlie knocked over his chair in his effort to keep

distance between him and the newcomer. Meredith was breathing heavily, but remained frozen in her seat.

"Who the hell —" Eshe said, turning back to the stranger.

Pointing a finger toward Charlie, who visibly twitched, Ule said, "I am, regrettably, an acquaintance of your friends there."

It clicked - and both Eshe and Hari shot up from their chairs. They looked about, looked at each other, and realised they were weaponless. Eshe grabbed her mug and brandished it.

Dinah sat transfixed. The stranger wasn't registering on her knack. He was giving off absolutely nothing.

"Ah, there is a little recognition from you, young witch," Ule said with an apologetic display of his teeth. He pointed slowly, even gently, to the tea tray as he crept forward like a child mimicking sneaking. "If I could request a parlay, perhaps with a calming brew?"

When he reached Eshe and Hari, he sidestepped them as if in a barn dance, and took the empty chair across from Dinah. There weren't enough cups, so he slid Charlie's from his vacated space and began to pour from the teapot.

"You killed our friend," Meredith said, anger and fear breaking the phrase into short bursts.

Ule nodded toward her as he set the teapot down. "Yes. Let's begin there. That is an accident for which I am most contrite, please believe me."

"An accident?" Dinah spat her words as if they were hot.

Eshe eyed her friend as if she might leap across

the table and scratch the stranger's eyes out of his head. She'd never seen Dinah annoyed, nevermind spitting angry, but Eshe had to admit that just under Dinah's milky surface was something scary. She caught movement in the corner of her eye, saw that Hari was edging toward the library's desk, but in his blind scrambling for a weapon he just knocked a stapler, ruler, and a few chewed pencils around.

The stranger seemed neither amused nor perturbed, not bothering to turn toward the racket.

"Yes, Dinah. I was trying to cover my escape, that I might have time to find my footing in this new era and decide what to do with my freedom. I have been incarcerated, you see. Wrongly. Tethered to the comet for over three hundred years as it hurtled through the void. Who knew that it would eventually bring me home again?" Ule turned sad, deep brown eyes on Dinah. "The mares should have never been deadly. You believe me, don't you?"

Hari stepped closer and Ule had to turn in his seat, mug in hand, to see the journalist brandishing a box of paperclips at him.

"Listen, mate. No way you're coming here pleading innocence. You killed someone. Accident or not. And our friends here are still having nightmares after meeting you for five seconds. That's pretty damning."

"You don't get put on a comet for three hundred years without reason," Eshe cut in. Behind Ule she could see Dinah making careful, swift movements with her hands. She dipped both middle fingers into her tea, wincing at the sting of the boiling water, drew parallel circles with the brew on the tabletop, and put her hands back down inside them as if she had never moved. Eshe had no idea what that meant, but it looked like she had prepared something.

Ule nodded. "It was a difference of opinion, followed by an overreaction. An impressive feat, really. Let it not be said that I cannot recognise genius, even in an enemy. Still, three centuries is too long to hold a grudge. I simply want to return home." He gestured as he spoke, and Eshe leaned away in case something came shooting out of his fingertips.

"Stop flopping your hands around. We don't know what you can do with them," she said.

In the name of peace, Ule turned back in his seat, knotting his fingers, and leant on the table.

Dinah's spell leapt to life and with a little puff of air that they all felt, Ule's knotted hands were fixed to the tabletop.

Dinah smiled but her eyes were a little too wild and unblinking for Eshe's liking.

Everyone moved at once. Hari grabbed the stranger's shoulders. Meredith shot up from her chair and punched Ule straight in the nose. He rocked back in his chair but was saved from falling backward by Dinah's spell locking his hands in place. Charlie grabbed for the phone and started to dial. And Eshe spun around to grab a sharpie from the desk.

Dagaunet sat perfectly still while chaos ensued, blood trickling down his upper lip. He didn't even look at Meredith who was still standing with her fists balled. He addressed Dinah. "A clever spell. What do you call it?"

"I- it doesn't have a name."

"Oh, you should always name your spells. I assume that you can't move your hands from the tabletop either. A mutual binding is risky. Now we're both stuck here."

"I have friends," Dinah said, but it came out sounding a little childish for her liking.

Ule's bottom lip tightened, conceding the point. He looked over his shoulder, and nodded acknowledgement to Hari as if they had just met in the street. By his feet, Eshe was drawing a circle and marking it with a little something to help Dinah hold the intruder in place.

"I'm not unreasonable nor a dullard," Ule continued, unfazed. "I know that you all are likely to have nothing in common with the witches who entrapped me. It has been a very long time. And I do not wish to make threats. Let us not speak of flayings, harrowing, and children boiled raw in the womb. The only answer I will not consider is 'no'. Otherwise, I'm willing to negotiate."

"For what?" Dinah asked. Under her feet she felt a tingle as Eshe's circle popped to life.

Ule continued to chat to Dinah as if the others weren't even there. "Kallin Beck. My terms are thus: I wish for you to leave the cottage so that I can reside there myself. The site was mine once and I would like it to be so again. I'm sure that you all understand. In return, you, yours, and this village will be unharmed. I'll give you three moons to think about what you would like in return and until the next full moon to vacate. I don't want anyone to be homeless or out of pocket and so all reasonable offers will be considered."

Dinah couldn't hide her confusion. "The cottage was yours?"

"Clarification. A reasonable request and, as you've seen, I am reasonable. Can we at least agree that I have been so? No amount of bloody noses will change that." Dinah didn't give an inch, so Ule carried on. "It was stolen from me. The cottage and its lands are rightfully mine by birthright. It was my mother's before me. However, I'm not saying that you can't come to visit Kallin Beck. I would not banish you. I have no friends in this era and would very much like to speak with you on the changes and modes in witchcraft and the world at large."

With a sigh, Ule stood, uncoupling and flexing his hands. The group shot back. Dinah's heart hammered with panic. The stranger had shrugged off her hasty shackle spell without a thought.

Smiling apologetically, Ule reached into his pocket, and with everyone frozen in surprise he produced a small, wrapped tablet of lead with a bronze nail hammered through it. Placing the defixio down on the table he tapped it with his index finger.

"Preparation," he said, before heading for the door.

Dinah's chair scraped back. "I don't need time to think —"

Ule held up a finger and Dinah's lips closed so hard that they made a sound.

"I urge you to take the time I have given you. Lest we return to the flaying, the harrowing, and those poor, poor babies. Three moons. And please remember that whatever happens was your chosen course, not mine. If you wish to reopen negotiations, I will be close at hand."

Eshe looked between her friend and the door, back and forth, back and forth, as Dagaunet disappeared into the street.

"Dinah? What do we do?"

Dinah was breathing heavily through her nose. Her lips were still glued shut. It took a few more seconds for the spell to wear off and for her to drag a huge breath into her lungs. Panting, she looked at Charlie who still had the phone in his hand, Theo's worried voice sounding shrill through the receiver.

"Charlie," Dinah said, panting, "You have to open the bochord."

CHAPTER TWENTY-THREE

Caillehall was as blunt up close as it seemed from afar. There wasn't a single adornment, decoration, or flair to the solid wood door, lattice windows, gables or grounds. There wasn't even a path up to the front door. It was as if no one had ever dared set foot that way. Isolde stood on the wide stone doorstep and lifted a hand to knock.

"What are you doing?" she muttered to herself, and turned the large iron handle at the door's centre.

Inside was as bland as out. The wooden floors were exquisitely maintained but bereft of rugs that might make the mansion more homely. The walls were covered in vintage floral wallpaper, but the designs had faded into the background until even Isolde had to really work to see them. In simple earthenware vases sprigs of dry wildflowers from the surrounding crags brought drab colours to the entrance hall.

Closing the door behind her as quietly as possible, Isolde crept further in, past the coat rack with only three black coats. Three pairs of old-style button boots stood underneath, varying only in size. There wasn't even space for a fourth pair. She looked down at her own boots, scuffed black DMs that hugged her feet.

Isolde thought of her heart as a coffin keepsake, unreachable and forgotten, but seeing once again that Amabel didn't even pretend to want her in the Tanner household brought a pebble to her throat that just wouldn't go down. She had to get back out of Caillehall as soon as possible. But she had to see Lucia and Vivian first.

The stairway was broad, lacquered dark wood. Isolde didn't even use the bannister, in case her mother sensed her touch in the old place, she just crept up one flight then up another, straight to the attic floor. There was no door to the attic room, just a jamb where the door should have been. Exposed beams drew Isolde's eye into the space, past row upon row of haphazardly stacked canvases lit by letterbox windows near the floor. At the end of the space, in a pool of baroque lighting from the larger gable window, a small figure in a long black dress had collapsed at the foot of a large easel, her arms still clinging to the half-finished image.

Isolde darted in, ignoring the hundreds of discarded artworks and the creaking floor that might give her away, and fell to her knees beside her younger sister. She grabbed Vivian by the shoulders finding that, despite the fact that she was unconscious, her hands maintained their death grip on the easel, so that they had to be pried free. Vivian fell back into Isolde's arms, her teenage face prematurely scarred by wrinkles around the eyes and mouth where she had squinted and scowled in her fervorous painting. Her hair was the same raven black as Isolde's but thick and wavy with what Isolde always thought of as vampiric lustre. Her beautiful silk dress was stained irredeemably with paint of every hue.

Vivian's eyes creaked open and she flinched in the light, only for her eyelids to fly open when she saw Isolde. She flung her arms around her sister, her fingers digging in painfully through Isolde's cut-off shirt.

"Isolde. Isolde. Are you here?"

"I'm here."

Vivian didn't look up, she just buried her face into her sister's chest. "Then what is the word? If it's really you."

"Diernan," Isolde said.

Vivian burst into sobs, her tears soaking through Isolde's shirt in an instant.

"I've been lost," Vivian whispered.

"I know."

"I tried to find my way back, but you weren't here. I tried to find my way to you, but you were in the water, and I couldn't reach you."

"I'm sorry, Viv. If I could have been here, you know I would have been."

"She sent you away."

"But I'm here now."

Vivian finally looked up, her glistening eyes wide and panicked. She glanced over Isolde's shoulder at the doorway, then back at her sister's worried face. "She'll find out."

"Let her," Isolde said.

"No-no-no. You should go again, and me with you this time. Maybe Lucia too. She poisons us, Isolde. Daily. The doses that she saved for you, she gives to us now."

Isolde avoided her sister's eyes. "Viv, you can't come with me. I have nowhere for you to go."

Vivian didn't answer, instead her eyes swivelled toward the doorway over Isolde's shoulder and fixed there. Isolde turned slowly to find another narrow black-clad figure in the dark aperture. With so many dark women walking the halls of Caillehall, it was no wonder that real ghosts stayed away.

Lucia walked toward them, a thin little book in her hand and her face soaked with pity. She took Vivian out of Isolde's arms, moving her carefully by the shoulders until the youngest sister was perched against a storage crate overflowing with canvases, legs splayed out across the boards, her face doll-like and perplexed.

"Don't worry, Vivian," Lucia whispered, stroking her sister's hair. "Everything is alright."

"Isolde was here," Vivian said, ignoring the fact that her sister was still sitting on the floor a few feet away.

Lucia nodded. Her voice came laced with a spell: "Rest a little. And then we'll read together."

Straight away, Vivian's head lolled, her hair falling across her face.

"You charmed her," Isolde said with shock.

Lucia stroked her youngest sister's hair. "It's the only way she sleeps now. And it won't last long. The visions startle her awake despite the magic. You shouldn't be here, Iz. You just feed into her delusions." Turning to Isolde, Lucia's face was soft and loving. "But I'm glad you've come. I miss you."

They embraced, kneeling on the creaking boards, until Lucia pulled away.

"Since you're here, you should eat something. Help me get Viv to the bed and then we'll talk downstairs."

Between them, they hoisted their little sister to a nearby futon piled high with blankets.

"But if Mother finds out —" Isolde said with a grunt of effort as she lifted Vivian's paint-stained bare feet onto the bed.

"She'll eat you? You're as bad as Viv, you really are. She can make a mountain flinch, but she's no monster, Iz."

Isolde scowled silently. Lucia took her hand and led her back down the stairs. They skirted through the dining room, past a large mahogany table and chairs, which were only used when Amabel hosted meetings with other witches, and straight to the kitchen where a more comfortable little table and chairs were waiting.

Lucia made sandwiches with cheese cut thick like a doorstop and bread sliced wonkily. She made terrible tea as well.

"Has she turned my room into a study yet?"

"She wouldn't do that."

"Then when will I be allowed to come home?"

"When the danger's passed."

"It never passes, Luce. There's always something on the horizon, some confluence or conjunction," Isolde said, dropping crumbs onto the table.

Lucia tutted, licked her finger, and dabbed up the crumbs.

"And that's why Mother needs you out there. Do you think she'd trust me or Viv to be out there unsupervised? And she couldn't do it herself. She'd see a TV in a shop window and run away like some startled caveman."

That brought a smile to Isolde's lips: the image of her mother screaming, arms flailing over her head as she hurtled through choked city streets.

"You're the Tanner most connected to the real world. Without you out there we'd be a myth, a mention only in certain circles."

"Why doesn't she just say that?" Isolde said, brandishing her sandwich.

"And show an emotion? The heavens would crack open." Lucia bit into her own diabolical cheese construction, chewing with her mouth daintily closed.

Isolde's chuckle faded swiftly. Putting her food aside, she said what was really on her mind. "Viv seems worse."

"Much," Lucia admitted. "She's rarely lucid now. Her paintings grow more abstract, frankly confounding Mother and myself. Useful premonitions are too difficult to pick out. We just dry and store them, give her fresh canvas, and hope that something snaps her back one day. If there's a way to help her, no one in our circle knows it. And believe me, we've asked everyone."

"She thinks Mother is poisoning her," Isolde said.

Lucia nodded.

"Isolde. You're home. I would show an emotion, but the heavens might crack open."

Isolde and Lucia didn't turn toward the kitchen

door where Amabel hung like some dark vision. They exchanged a tense glance instead, Isolde clenching her teeth in a caught-in-the-act grimace, and Lucia mouthing, “Oops”.

Chapter Twenty-Four

Dinah couldn't shake the feeling that she should have been brandishing a flaming torch as she followed Charlie down the library's cellar corridor. They passed through the archives room, a huge panel of breaker switches, and a boiler that had seen world wars come and go. The walls became old stone, the path a gentle slope that took left turn after left turn, as if they were circling down under the library.

"Dinah, what the hell is this?" Eshe asked, whispering over Dinah's shoulder for some reason. "If you have a magic bunker, we really could have used that earlier."

"Not a bunker," Dinah whispered back. "Nana Haigh called it her bochord. I've only been in here once myself."

Up ahead, Charlie unlocked an old wooden door and they passed through in single file, with Hari coming last. When they were all in, Charlie closed the door behind them. They all stood in pitch darkness for a second before a series of wall-mounted lamps all around the room fizzed to life. It was impossible to see how large the space was. Bookshelves built of rough wood blocked line of sight in all directions, the shelves laid out as haphazardly as the lighting, everything feeling like it had been added as an afterthought rather than as part of some grand design. There were crevices and nooks everywhere, some pitch black and some brightly lit. Mismatched chairs and little tables poked out of the odd alcoves. And on the shelves were hundreds and hundreds of books in all sizes and styles and bindings.

"A library under the library," Meredith said.

"You know librarians are natural kleptos," Charlie said, his tone not rising to the joke.

Hari just looked around himself for a moment in silence. "This place is insane. The whole town. All this stuff about magic —"

Eshe gripped his shoulder gently. "Yeah. Tell me about it."

Dinah stepped forward. The shelves nearest to the door were mostly empty, holding only a few books with relatively new covers and bindings.

"The further in you go, the older the books get," she said quietly.

"How far back do they go?" Eshe said, peering into the gloom with excitement.

Dinah gave her a wan smile. "Very. But we need to focus, right?"

"Three days to find something of use in this huge

collection," Charlie said. "Piece of cake if it was in some kind of order other than vaguely chronological. Or if they were marked in some way." Under his breath, he added, "Dewey would have a stroke."

"They're not in order?" Meredith asked. She looked like she might have a stroke herself.

Charlie shook his head, giving Dinah a sidelong look. "They're not my books to mess with. And I don't think I'd know what I was looking at even if I read them."

"We have a name and a century," Hari added, tracing his fingers along a stacked shelf. "It's a start, but not much of one, mind."

"Charlie —" Dinah started to say, but he cut her off.

"I know, I know. I'll put the kettle on."

Vivian gave little grunts of effort that seemed excessive for the work of shepherding paint. Lucia had been right; her charm had lasted less than an hour and they had heard Vivian moving around in the attic room again. Isolde watched her sister move with listless grace around her canvas. She had foregone using brushes now. From her fingertips to her wrists, her skin was covered in layers of paint as she manipulated the colours with her bare hands. This was the worst that Isolde had ever seen her in terms of both exhaustion and her grip on the present.

The older sisters moved around the attic space, pulling canvases out of storage, putting some aside and returning others, all under the watchful eye of their mother. At one end of the room, they stacked the paintings of things they knew had already happened. What remained were uncertain visions of all kinds.

Lifting a smaller canvas from a box, Isolde regarded the portrait with no less wonder than she had Vivian's first premonition when she had been just a little girl with crayons. This portrait was of Isolde herself, on a lumpy sofa, a rough wool blanket over her knees. Isolde knew that room. It was the living room at Kallin Beck. The image was of the night she'd spent guarding the cottage with Eshe. She looked at herself again, her face was pensive yet peaceful. A little dawn light came through the unseen window glinting from the knick-knacks on the shelves beside her and warming her pale skin to a glow.

Another painting was of Isolde again, sitting in the midground of a moonlit bus station. Isolde knew the place by the iron and glass awning she was sitting under. Whitby. That had been over a year ago. Vivian always made her look prettier than she was, she thought. A sister's loving gaze warping the truth.

She removed both paintings to the end of the room devoted to the past.

Lucia had also been putting Vivian's most recently completed works together in a small gallery stacked against one wall. Amabel was staring at them.

"These are the hardest to discern," she said with the hint of emotion so small that only her girls would be able to recognise it. "Her visions are becoming less vivid as she slips further from us."

She was right that Vivian's style had changed. The portrait that Isolde had put aside was a contemporary oil painting with few visible strokes and expertly composed lighting. The newest were more Impressionist with forms blurring to the point of abstraction.

"No," Isolde said, the habit of contradicting her mother coming easily to her. "Not less vivid, more profound. She used to just make a copy of what she saw. They might as well have been a photograph. Now it's as if she's really there. She feels it. She's conveying the emotions as well."

Amabel's head barely turned toward Isolde. From the corner of her eye, she regarded her middle child, but she didn't argue.

Isolde tried to ignore the look, instead keeping her attention on Vivian's paintings. Where Amabel and Lucia had no frame of reference for anywhere outside of Caillehall, Isolde occasionally recognised some of the painted scenes. At least the places, even if she had no idea when the events would happen.

The first image's chunky strokes conveyed much with very little. Verdant greens ran down either side of the canvas. Grey forms with curlicues of white flowed down the centre. Unless you had stood on the banks of Kallin Beck with your own two feet, it would have been impossible to tell that this was an image of the stream and the transparent ripples flowing over the smooth stones at its bottom. It was a perfect representation of the feeling Isolde got staring down into the beck near the cottage. But if she looked closer, she could see the faintest elements of pink, red, and then scarlet leaking into the image at the very top, like blood in the water.

She moved on swiftly.

Edge to edge the next canvas was filled with climbing coils in charcoal hues and the faintest licks of red and ochre. Isolde could almost feel heat coming from it and she recognised what it was right away. It was as if Vivian had painted the smoke of a fire but had forgotten to paint in the objects that it flowed around, leaving only a suggestion of place from the forms that the smoke took. Isolde knew the room. Bookshelves, a table, a desk. More smoke poured from an unseen door at the back of the room that she could see only by the way the black coils licked some rectangular aperture. And on the floor of the Hexford library, soot and ash piled on a prone human figure.

Something came over Isolde that she never usually felt. She shuddered. The sensation scared her more than the picture.

"Done," Vivian whispered to herself, yanking their attention toward her. She slid the painting from the easel with one hand, letting it clatter to the ground with a crack of its wooden frame. Without pause, she made her way to the pile of fresh canvases - but she only made it halfway before her knees buckled. She crawled instead, until her dirty fingers found the edge of the next canvas and she dragged it toward her across the floor.

Lucia and Isolde darted forward to catch their sister, Lucia grabbing her shoulders, Isolde brushing aside her hair to see the ashen face beneath. As they held her back from the canvas, Vivian groaned like a child, reaching out, trying to fight them off, but there was no energy left in her and she flopped down, defeated.

Lucia whispered sweet charms into her sister's ear and in a moment Vivian had settled.

Isolde looked up at their mother, who stood stock still and staring at her youngest daughter.

"She can't keep this up, Mother," she said.

Amabel said nothing but Isolde caught the faint

flicker of sadness in her mother's eyes before all composure was restored. If her mother was going to start showing human emotions, Isolde might have to change her ire to pity. She wasn't sure she was ready for that.

She pushed on. "We have to get her to bed. Properly, this time. Down to her own room and out of this place. Luce, what do you think?"

Lucia was still singing soft charms in Vivian's ear, and so she just nodded.

"No," Amabel said. Isolde's anger threatened to boil over, but as she took a breath to shout her mother down, Amabel finished her thought, "Let me take her."

She swept down to pluck Vivian from her sisters' arms. Despite her thin frame, Amabel took her daughter's weight with ease and bore her away without another word, Vivian muttering and twitching in her uneasy sleep.

Isolde watched, astonished at the display of maternal care that she couldn't remember ever seeing before. She had certainly never been on the receiving end of it. She shrugged that off, putting it in a little box labelled with a lie - I don't care - and turned her attention to Vivian's discarded painting where it lay on the ground.

In pale greys edged with darkest shades, Vivian had managed to convey the feeling of being under water with every stroke of movement. Black, sunken branches encroached on the scene from each side. Moonlight rippled on the distant, shimmering surface. Isolde knew the place straight away. It was the view from the bottom of the lake where she went in her meditations. She knew it by the moonlight shafts that she loved to watch dance through the dark water. But in the centre of the image, staring down in the water, floated a pale body with a shock of wild silver hair around its head. Fossegrim, face down, impossibly drowned in his own lake.

Isolde tore her eyes away from the form of the dead spirit, only for them to pass over more of Vivian's paintings. Now she had seen some, it was obvious what the others were. All of them were of Hexford. The High Street smothered by a maelstrom, gnarled and charred ruins in the footprint of Kallin Beck cottage - and more, so many more. All images of death and destruction for the places and people she had so recently met.

"Goddess, what is happening?" she whispered.

Epilogue

The others were all somewhere in the bochord, all out of sight, but Dinah could feel them with her knack, moving around, stirring the stale air. None of them knew where to start, of course, neither in the shelves or in the task ahead. But they had to start somewhere and so they had spread out. She heard them occasionally too, whispering to one another. She smiled to herself. How odd that people, both magical and not, paid the space such reverence.

Dinah wished that her mother's book had been there, but of course it was with her on her travels. A shudder ran through her so fiercely that she hugged herself. She looked at the shelf beside her; one of the more recent ones that was yet to be entirely filled. She wondered whether her own recipe book would end up there one day, and if anyone would ever read it. There was one book on the last shelf that caught her eye. Its spine hung off at an odd angle to show the stitches and glue underneath. Using both hands to support the binding, she took it down. It had been a beautiful teal leather tome at some point with gilded writing on the cover. But it was easy to see that it had been water damaged, forcing the cover to warp, and the pages to crinkle and splay.

Dinah knew this book. As she ran her hands over the cover, she knew that she'd done it before. She remembered the feel of the leather. A smell came back to her. Lavender on the breeze. She cracked open the book to find a sprig of pressed lavender tucked into the inside cover. Many of the pods had fallen off over the years and they slid off the book to bounce off Dinah's toes. Still, the smell was strong, and Dinah's palms tingled with the sensation of rubbing fresh lavender between them to activate the scent.

This was Nana Haigh's book.

A lump rose in her throat, making it hard to breathe. Dinah didn't want to cry, so she swallowed the sensation down. Still, her eyes burned with the threat of tears as she turned the first loose page.

A recipe. The first page was a recipe for a tea, surrounded with bleeding ink and pigment that might have once been watercolour illustrations.

Dinah stroked the page, and she breathed through the urge to weep, her lungs filling with the scent of lavender again. She turned the page. Another recipe, this time for grilled cheese, then herby potatoes, and something called 'Beltane Brew'. Dinah went slowly so as not to disturb the damaged tome, but her fingers were shaking. Nana Haigh's spellbook was a recipe book, just like hers. And hadn't her nan been respected? Hell, her mother had told Dinah that Nana Haigh was even feared in certain circles. Dinah turned another page to find a series of bouquet garni with different effects but some of the ingredients had been lost to the water. She had protected Kallin Beck and Hexford with nothing but handfuls of herbs and bags of flour. Just like Dinah. She closed the book, ran her fingers down the leather cover again, and wiped away an errant tear with the sleeve of her cardigan.

"Thanks, Nan."

Eshe poked her head around a bookcase and tugged down her glasses. "You ok?"

"Yeah. Just thinking."

Stepping out from behind the bookshelf, Eshe leant with her arms folded, head tilted to rest on the shelf next to her, but she didn't say anything.

"We can do this, you know," Dinah said. To her surprise, she actually meant it. She chuckled. "You and me, and this lot of troublemakers."

"Yeah."

"You know, if you still don't want to be involved-" Dinah started.

"Oh, I'm involved." Eshe said as she stared at a spot somewhere beyond the bookcases. "I was just being a 'fraidy cat before. I was overwhelmed, you know?"

"I can't remember the last time I was just regularly whelmed."

That pulled a laugh from Eshe.

"I'm in this with you. I've seen stuff I never thought I would. I've done magic I thought I'd only ever write about and - this is mental - I like it. I've felt hopeless a lot of times in my life, D. I've been scared. Really scared. When we were facing that thing in Meredith's bedroom, I was just kind of shocked, not really scared. Because you were there with me. And then when Dagaunet was sitting right there in front of us, I wasn't scared either. The magic just— I don't know."

"You were really brave. I was dying inside the whole time." Dinah admitted.

Eshe turned to her friend and took her hand. "It feels good to be doing magic, to be protecting this place, and to be here with you. I want to be here."

Dinah threw herself into Eshe's arms.

"We'll be ok," Dinah said, her voice muffled by Eshe's knitted vest.

Sitting on the crumbling dry stone wall that marked the boundary of Kallin Beck cottage's garden, Ule Dagaunet felt good. The moon was high, the night was clear, and he was close, oh so close, to home.

The cottage itself hadn't changed a bit. Neither in looks nor demeanour. Ule poked his tongue out at the drooping roofs and wonky windows, and felt the cottage gnash its teeth.

"Oh, hush," he said.

The stream itself was silent. He was grateful for that. But everything else, down to the smell of sheep dung on the breeze, was exactly as it had been. All he had to do was get inside - and that would happen in no time at all.

Perched there by moonlight, a contented sigh parted his lips, and Ule Dagaunet sang in an off-key baritone:

There were three ravens sat on a tree,
Down-a-down, hey down, hey down.
They were black as black could be, with a down.
Then one of them said to his mate:
"Where shall we our breakfast take?"
With a down, derry derry derry, down, down.

Down in yonder green field,
Down-a-down, hey down, hey down.
There lies a knight slain under his shield, with a down.
Down there comes a fallow doe,
As great with young as she might go,
With a down, derry derry derry, down, down.

She lifted up his bloody head,
Down-a-down, hey down, hey down.
And kissed his wounds that were so red, with a down.
She buried him before the prime,
She was dead herself, ere even-song time
With a down, derry derry derry, down, down.

The Hexford Witches will return in:

No Illusions

Coming Soon!

Dinah's Home-from-home Scones

500g Strong white flour
50g Unsalted butter
80g Caster Sugar
5tsp Baking Powder
3 medium eggs
250ml Whole Milk

1. Preheat oven to 220°C
2. Mix butter and flour together in a bowl until you get a crumbly texture.
3. Add castor sugar and baking powder and mix.
4. Add two eggs and gently mix in.

5. Add in the milk and mix until you have a soft paste.
6. Taking your mixture out of the bowl, spread some flour on your counter and fold the mixture together.
7. Roll out the mixture into a thick patty of about 1 inch depth. Flour your scone cutter (Dinah uses a glass tumbler) and cut your scones.
8. Put some baking paper onto a baking tray and place your cut scones onto it.
9. Break and whisk an egg into a bowl and paint the scone tops with it.
10. Put your baking tray in the oven and cook for fifteen minutes. Just long enough for a cup of tea.

Nana Haigh's Hot Milk

1 cup milk
1 teaspoon vanilla extract
2 tablespoons white sugar
¼ teaspoon ground nutmeg

1. In a small bowl, stir together the milk, vanilla and sugar.
2. Warm the milk in a saucepan over a medium heat, stirring continuously.
3. Transfer to your favourite mug and stir in nutmeg.
4. Serve hot.

Dinah's Third Eye Dredge

1 teaspoon paprika
¼ teaspoon ground black pepper
1 teaspoon onion powder
1 teaspoon garlic
¼ teaspoon cayenne pepper
1 teaspoon oregano
½ teaspoon salt

1. Mix all ingredients together in a jar, tub or bowl. No cooking required. Save for invisible emergencies or for chicken that needs tasty seasoning.

Threshold Bolster Jars

Vinegar
Garlic
Salt
Rosemary
Cinnamon stick
A Basil leaf
Star Anise

1. Place your herbs together in a sealable container.
2. Pour over the vinegar until your ingredients are all submerged.
3. Seal your container tight and add any charms or sigils that you wish.
4. Place your jar in a high place, preferably near a door or window.

ABOUT THE AUTHOR

C.B. Hallam is an international best-selling author from Doncaster, UK. His work spans all aspects of Speculative Fiction and Mental Health non-fiction, and poetry.

Since his debut in the British Fantasy Society journal, his tales have nestled between the pages of magazines and anthologies the world over. His novels and short stories have filled the imaginations of geeks, niche and alternative readers with their character-driven style and unusual plots.

Writing as Craig Hallam, he has written in genres as diverse as Steampunk (The *Alan Shaw* trilogy), horror (*Emi*), and non-binary dystopian cyberpunk (*Oshibana Complex*). He chronicled his experiences of living with depression and anxiety in the international best-seller, *Down Days*, which topped the Amazon charts in the UK and US at the start of 2020. The book has since been a finalist for the Independent Author Network's Book of the Year Awards and has been read the world over.

Find Craig's books and social media at:
Linktr.ee/craighallamauthor

Praise for Craig Hallam:
"A considered dismantling of the macho hero archetype."
Nimue Brown, author of *Hopeless Maine*

"Witty, expressive and rich."
Biff Raven-Hill

"A kick in the shinplates to more stereotypical fare."
Steampunk Chronicle

"Atmospheric...darkly visceral"
The Byproduct

"Sharp, sardonic wit that is unmistakably British"
Nathan Robinson, author of *Ketchup On Everything, Starers, Caldera*

Printed in Great Britain
by Amazon

53539240R00106